The truth was that she'd got to him.

On some visceral level. From the moment he'd seen her camera lens pointed straight at him, provoking an extreme reaction. Not everyone would have reacted the way he had. His brother Nikos would have smiled and posed.

For Maks, though, camera lenses represented intrusions of privacy, and he'd spent the last two weeks wondering if he'd massively overreacted. A knee-jerk reaction to old traumas.

Yet, when he'd seen her this evening, the mere sight of her had sparked that visceral reaction again. A need to see her up close, juxtaposed with a need to push her away. And this time she hadn't even had a camera. *Because you took it.*

Whatever it was about the way she made him react, he knew he couldn't let her walk away again. As much because he owed her this apology as for other, deeper and less coherent reasons. *Because you want her*, whispered a voice. He ignored it. She'd taken her hair down, but it couldn't hide her exquisite bone structure or delicate beauty. Or the scars. The one above her lip and the other one at her cheek. He wanted to reach out and trace them.

Abby Green

THE INNOCENT BEHIND
THE SCANDAL

Recycling programs
for this product may
not exist in your area.

ISBN-13: 978-1-335-14908-4

The Innocent Behind the Scandal

Copyright © 2020 by Abby Green

All rights reserved. No part of this book may be used or reproduced in
any manner whatsoever without written permission except in the case of
brief quotations embodied in critical articles and reviews.

This is a work of fiction. Names, characters, places and incidents
are either the product of the author's imagination or are used fictitiously.
Any resemblance to actual persons, living or dead, businesses,
companies, events or locales is entirely coincidental.

This edition published by arrangement with Harlequin Books S.A.

For questions and comments about the quality of this book,
please contact us at CustomerService@Harlequin.com.

Harlequin Enterprises ULC
22 Adelaide St. West, 40th Floor
Toronto, Ontario M5H 4E3, Canada
www.Harlequin.com

Printed in U.S.A.

Irish author **Abby Green** ended a very glamorous career in film and TV—which really consisted of a lot of standing in the rain outside actors' trailers—to pursue her love of romance. After she'd bombarded Harlequin with manuscripts they kindly accepted one, and an author was born. She lives in Dublin, Ireland, and loves any excuse for distraction. Visit abby-green.com or email abbygreenauthor@gmail.com.

Books by Abby Green

Harlequin Presents

The Virgin's Debt to Pay
Awakened by the Scarred Italian
The Greek's Unknown Bride

Conveniently Wed!

Claiming His Wedding Night Consequence

One Night With Consequences

An Innocent, A Seduction, A Secret

The Marchetti Dynasty

The Maid's Best Kept Secret

Rival Spanish Brothers

Confessions of a Pregnant Cinderella
Redeemed by His Stolen Bride

Visit the Author Profile page
at Harlequin.com for more titles.

I'd like to dedicate this book to Annie West, who is not only one of my favourite romance authors, but, I'm honoured to say, my friend. We sold to Harlequin around the same time and our first books hit the shelves within months of each other.

Since those first books she has provided support, much-needed advice and friendship. Not to mention inspiration! She helped ease my path into becoming a writer and took the terror out of navigating a whole new world.

Thank you, Annie. This is for you. xx

CHAPTER ONE

Paris

HE WAS THE most beautiful man Zoe Collins had ever seen, and that was some realisation when she was currently surrounded by some of the world's most physically perfect men and women at one of Paris Fashion Week's biggest shows.

He was sitting in the front row, so he had to be important.

Aware that she was staring, Zoe dragged her gaze away and looked around the vast ballroom that had been transformed into a fairy woodland scene, with real trees down the centre of the catwalk. The air was scented with the expensive perfume of the hundreds of guests milling around while they waited for the show to start.

Her heart was still pounding from the adrenalin rush of what she'd just done.

She'd been outside the Grand Palais, taking pictures of 'influencers' as they went into the show, and by pure fluke she'd noticed one of the catering staff outside a door, having a cigarette. When he went back inside he'd left the door ajar, and Zoe had seized the opportunity to get into the inner sanctum.

She knew that if she could actually manage to get into 'the pit', where the official photographers lined themselves up at the end of the catwalk, she would be able to try and convince them that she was one of them. Even though she wasn't. At all. She was a self-taught amateur photographer.

There was no way she would have got accreditation to be in here officially. As it was, some of the other photographers were looking at her suspiciously. She hunched forward, letting her shoulder-length hair hide her face, and hoped they wouldn't notice that she had no official lanyard.

Excitement buzzed under her skin. She'd never been at a fashion show before, and it had always been a dream of hers to see the spectacle up close. Along with the dream becoming a bona fide fashion photographer. For as long as she could remember she'd escaped into glossy magazines and pored for hours over the fantastical editorial created by the industry's best photographers, editors and stylists.

But breaking into a tight-knit industry like this was akin to climbing Everest without oxygen. Next to impossible without contacts or experience.

She knew she shouldn't draw attention to herself, but she couldn't resist looking at the man again. When her gaze found him her pulse-rate skipped and her heart beat a little faster.

He had more than just good looks, she realised. There was an air of impenetrability about him. He was talking to no one. Looking at no one. Glancing down periodically at his phone. Totally relaxed, yet primed. Interested, but not showing interest. Aloof.

She guessed he was tall, just from the way he dominated the space around him. He had broad shoulders, a lean body. Very short hair—almost militarily short. Dark under the lights, but not brown, or black. More dark blond.

But his bone structure alone had Zoe lifting the camera to her face, almost without realising what she was doing. And when she looked through her viewfinder her heart stopped altogether.

Close up, he wasn't just beautiful—he was breathtaking. High cheekbones, deep-set eyes. A mouth that promised decadence and sin. Firm contours. Sensual. A hard, uncompromising jaw that a shadow of stubble only enhanced.

There was a faintly olive tone to his skin. And then his head turned and his eyes connected directly with hers through her camera. She froze. His eyes were mesmerising. Dark grey. Cold. Cynical. Guarded.

Zoe acted on instinct. Her finger came down on the button and the camera made a clicking sound as it immortalised his image for ever.

But before she could even take the camera down from her face there was a blur of movement, and then she was being grabbed by her jacket and hauled up and out of the pit full of photographers.

'Who the hell are you and why are you taking pictures of me?'

Dimly, Zoe recognised the fact that his voice matched the rest of him. Deep and authoritative. Slightly accented. She also recognised that he was much taller than she might have guessed. Well over six feet, and towering over her own far less substantial five foot four.

His eyes raked her up and down. 'Who are you? Where's your accreditation?'

'I…' She faltered, all the bravado that had led her in here dissolving. She swallowed. 'I don't have any.'

She vaguely heard muttering from the other photographers and guilty heat climbed up over her chest to her face.

'Look, I'm sorry. I saw an open door and I just—'

'Thought you'd enter illegally?'

Zoe spluttered. 'Well, that's a bit extreme, isn't it?'

He put his hand on her arm and pulled her out of the photographers' area and along the front row towards the main doors, on the opposite side of the room from where she'd entered. Her face burned with humiliation. Who the hell did this guy think he was? Acting like judge and jury? Crashing a fashion show was hardly the crime of the century!

Zoe could see people tucking their legs out of the way as they passed, and noted several iconic famous faces assuming looks of disgust and horror as she was all but hauled out.

When they were on the other side of the main doors she pulled free. She could see security guards approaching, but the man put up a hand and they stopped. She looked up, breathless. Adrenalin rushed through her system, and something else—something that felt disturbingly like excitement.

'Who *are* you?' She rubbed her arm, even though he hadn't hurt her at all.

He didn't answer, just reached for her camera, lifting it over her head before she could stop him.

She reacted instantly, reaching for it. 'Hey, that's my camera. You can't just—'

But a hand planted squarely on her upper chest, holding her back, stopped her words.

She watched in dismay as he easily accessed and scrolled through the pictures, presumably finding the one of him, and the ones she'd taken outside.

He closed one hand around the camera and took his other hand down from her chest. 'I'll take this. You can go.'

Zoe went cold inside. 'But you can't just take my camera—that's my property.'

Her most precious possession.

It had belonged to her father and it had gone everywhere with her since that awful—

She spoke rapidly to push down unwelcome memories. She didn't need those now. 'Are you Security? You can wipe all the pictures. I don't care. Just please give me back the camera.' She put out her hand. Panicking.

The man's voice was incredulous. 'You don't know who I am?'

She looked at him. She wasn't all that up to date on pop culture or gossip magazines, but she was fairly sure he wasn't an actor or a singer. Although he did look vaguely familiar. Maybe he was a male model. He certainly had the looks. Although there was something raw about him—as if he would never do anything so submissive as pose for a photograph.

'You're *not* Security?'

'I'm Maks Marchetti.'

He looked at her. She looked at him. Shock spread through her body.

Maks Marchetti.

He arched a brow. 'The Marchetti Group? We own the fashion house whose show you just crashed.'

Zoe could feel the blood draining south from her face. Faintly she said, 'I know who you are.'

The reason she hadn't recognised him was because he was the most reclusive of the three Marchetti brothers, who had inherited the business from their father on his death some years previously.

The Marchetti Group was at the very top end of exclusive, and had become even more so in the years since Marchetti Senior's death. It owned every major brand in the world—and if they didn't own it they were busy acquiring it. The brands they didn't own weren't worth mentioning.

And this man was a Marchetti. Which meant he could buy and sell everyone in that room.

She could hear music starting now. Presumably the show was kicking off. That dark grey gaze was unnervingly direct. He seemed unconcerned that he was missing the start. Zoe recalled that sense of aloofness she'd picked up from him.

'Shouldn't you be inside? If you could just give me back the camera I'll go and you'll never see me again.'

Maks Marchetti looked down at the woman in front of him, more transfixed than he liked to admit. At first glance she was pretty average. Average height, average weight and build. Slim. Petite, actually. But there was something about her that kept him looking—that had caught his attention when he'd looked over and seen the camera raised to her face, pointing directly at him.

She had honey-blonde shoulder-length hair. Finely etched brows. A delicate jaw. Straight nose. Her eyes were an arresting shade of green and blue. Aquamarine. Pretty.

More than pretty, actually.

But she had a scar—an indentation that dissected her top lip on one side, almost an inch long. There was another scar too, that ran from one upper cheekbone to under her hairline. They piqued his interest.

As if sensing his gaze on her, she ducked her head and her hair fell forward, covering her face. 'It's rude to stare.'

Maks had to curb an impulse to reach out and tip up her chin so he could see her. She was a complete stranger.

'It's rude to trespass.'

She looked up again, those eyes flashing green. They were long-lashed. She wore no make-up that he could see and her skin was flawless. Apart from the scars. It was the colour of pale cream roses with a hint of pink. It made him wonder what she would look like in the throes of passion. Would her eyes turn a deeper green when she was aroused? Would her cheeks flush a deeper pink?

An unexpected jolt of lust caught him by surprise. More than a jolt. Actually, she wasn't just pretty. She was beautiful—but in a way that crept up on him. He moved in a world that celebrated beauty so much that he'd almost become inured to it. But she had a kind of beauty he'd never seen before. Understated. Captivating.

Dio. What the hell was wrong with him?

He took a step back. 'Leave now and I won't have you prosecuted for trespassing.'

She went pale.

He ignored his conscience. 'We don't allow paparazzi into our shows.'

Her mouth opened and he noticed her lips. Wide and lush. Soft. Tempting. His eye was drawn to that intriguing scar again.

'I am *not* paparazzi.'

She'd drawn herself up, her whole body quivering as if she was indignant. Maks had to hand it to her: she was a good actress. He ignored the way he wanted to drop his gaze down over her body and study her more thoroughly. There was a distinct hum in his blood now and he did not welcome this distraction. Or attraction...

'Well, I'm afraid that sneaking into one of the biggest shows of the season, with wall-to-wall A-list guests, makes me a touch suspicious. And in any case this is not up for discussion.'

Maks Marchetti looked over her head and made a gesture. Zoe turned around to see two beefy security men approaching them. She swivelled back to Marchetti. 'Look, please, I didn't mean any harm. I'm really not paparazzi.'

But her words fell on deaf ears.

Marchetti said over her head, 'Please escort this young woman out. Make sure she doesn't ever get into another show again.'

Zoe's mouth fell open as her arms were taken on each side, lightly but firmly. She glared at Marchetti.

How had she thought he was beautiful? The man was cruel and cold.

'Seriously? You're blacklisting me?'

Now she wouldn't get in even if she had a lanyard. Her dreams of breaking into the lower echelons of the fashion photography industry were going up in smoke.

The security guards started to lead her away. She saw her camera dangling carelessly from Marchetti's hand. 'What about my camera?'

He held it up. 'You lost it the moment you trespassed. Goodbye. I hope we don't meet again, for your sake.'

Zoe was being propelled backwards, and she knew she should turn around. She didn't even know this man and she'd gone from thinking he was gorgeous to hating him all within a few seismic minutes. But she couldn't tear her gaze from his.

And, worse, there was a feeling of...*hurt* at what he'd said. That he hoped they wouldn't meet again. What on earth was that about?

It galvanised her to say, 'Well, for what it's worth, Mr Marchetti, you're the last man on earth that *I* ever want to meet again.'

He lifted a hand—the one without her camera. He even let his mouth tip up at one corner. *'Ciao.'*

Maks watched the security men take the woman outside and disappear. It was crazy, but for a moment he'd almost wanted to go after them and tell them to let her go.

And do what? he scoffed at himself. *Look at her some more?*

He shook his head and went back into the show.

He watched it from the back of the room, barely

taking in the rapturous applause at the end. And, even though he'd just watched some of the world's most beautiful women parade down a catwalk in front of him, he couldn't seem to get a pair of long-lashed aquamarine eyes out of his head.

He went still inside, though, when he realised that he hadn't even taken her name. She'd distracted him that much. He scowled. Just as well he'd ensured she wouldn't gain access again. He didn't need distractions like her.

Maks looked at the camera in his hand. It was an old Nikon, probably about twenty years old, and a bit battered. There was a bin nearby, and he knew he should just throw it away and put that brief encounter out of his head, say good riddance to the whole encounter. He wouldn't see her ever again.

A few hours later, Zoe looked broodingly out of the window of the train as it arrived back into London. Early autumn had been sunny in Paris, but London's late-afternoon skies were leaden and did little to elevate her mood. Every time she thought of that last image of Maks Marchetti, smirking and saying *ciao* with her camera dangling from his hand, she wanted to scream—or cry.

To her horror, tears prickled behind her eyelids. How could she have lost her beloved father's camera like that? It was probably at the bottom of a rubbish bin by now. Wiped clean of all pictures. Memory card destroyed.

Absently she touched the scar above her lip. It was that camera that had given her the scar. Both scars.

When their car had crashed seventeen years ago, killing her parents and her younger brother. She'd been eight. Ben had been five. Her parents had been in their prime.

She'd been holding the camera in her hands and her father had looked back at her for a moment, telling her to be careful with it. And then… Then the world had exploded in a ball of fire and pain and her life had changed overnight. She'd become an orphan. She and the camera were the only things that had survived the crash.

Zoe took her hand down from her mouth and squeezed her eyes shut, as if that might block out the unwelcome memories. She did not need to go there now. She went there enough in her dreams and nightmares.

She opened her eyes again and forced emotion out. It was entirely her fault she'd lost her father's camera. She shouldn't have been so impulsive. If it hadn't been for that other photographer telling her that if she could get into an actual show then she might have a real chance to make some decent contacts then she wouldn't even have thought of it.

A frisson ran over her skin when she thought about the man. Maks Marchetti. He'd been so…intense. Overwhelming. She had to acknowledge now that, in spite of the stress of the situation which she'd found herself in—entirely her own fault—she'd felt alive in a way that had had nothing to do with the adrenalin running through her body.

He'd looked at her scars. Everyone did after a few seconds, when they registered them. She was used to the skin-prickling moment when eyes widened and then narrowed, followed by a quick look at her eyes to see if she'd noticed. Then a guilty or apologetic smile. Embarrassment.

Zoe knew she was lucky. Her scars weren't *that* disfiguring. But when Maks Marchetti had looked at them she hadn't felt the usual sense of invasion. She'd ducked her head because, disturbingly, she'd felt something else—awareness.

Zoe went cold inside. The same kind of awareness that had led her into trusting someone who had betrayed her trust. Who had almost done a lot worse than just betray her trust.

The train slowed down and Zoe clamped down on her rogue thoughts again, welcoming the sight of the station ahead.

She wasn't as naive as she had been before. Now if a man affected her she was doubly wary, because she knew how awareness, or desire, could hide the truth about someone until it was almost too late.

The train drew to a stop inside St Pancras Station.

She couldn't help wondering, though… If she knew better now, then why did she feel a sense of loss at the fact that she'd never meet Maks Marchetti again?

It was ridiculous. Right now he was presumably at a glamorous after-party, while Zoe was headed towards the labyrinthine Tube system to get back to her tiny East London flat. Their worlds couldn't be further apart. She was scarred—on the outside and the inside. He was not.

She'd learnt her lesson in attempting to infiltrate a world that was not open to her. The truth was that her love of photography was just a hobby—a hobby that was now getting her into trouble. The prospect of it ever becoming anything more seemed further away than ever. In the meantime, she had a living to earn.

Two weeks later, London

Zoe's arms ached, and her face ached even more from fake smiling. Her tray went from heavy to light and then heavy again, in relentless rotation, as she passed around glasses of champagne to the glittering *crème de la crème* of London's most famous and beautiful.

In an ironic twist of fate, the catering company she worked part-time for was catering a fashion event. The launch of a new head designer at a famous fashion house. It was being held in their flagship shop on Bond Street. And the label was owned by the Marchetti Group, of course.

Zoe felt the back of her neck prickle, but brushed the sensation away. She blamed it on her hair being tied up—a rule of the job. She always felt more exposed when it was up. Exposed, and then guilty for feeling exposed. Her scars were a reminder, after all, of the incident that had defined her life.

She told herself off for feeling paranoid. Maks Marchetti was in Paris. He was hardly likely to turn up at every event the group presided over.

Pushing him firmly from her mind, she turned and faced the other way for a bit, hoping her tray would lighten soon.

And then she spotted someone across the room and her blood ran cold. A tall man. Broad. Short hair glinting dark blond under the lights. He wore a steel-grey suit, a white shirt open at the neck. He was holding a half-empty glass of champagne carelessly in one hand. His head was bent towards a tall, statuesque red-haired woman who was wearing a very short, very sparkly green dress, who had the longest legs Zoe had ever seen.

It was him.

As if sensing Zoe looking at him, he lifted his head and those all too familiar dark grey eyes met hers before she could even move. His gaze narrowed. Recognition dawned and his expression turned icy.

Zoe could practically read his lips. *What the hell is she doing here?* He said something else to the woman, never taking his gaze off Zoe, pinning her to the spot, and then came towards her, putting his glass down on a table.

She couldn't move. Like a deer caught in a car's headlights. He stopped right in front of her. She'd convinced herself over the last couple of weeks that he couldn't possibly be as beautiful as she remembered. But he was. Devastatingly so. Even if he was horrible and cruel.

'How did *you* get in here?'

'I'm working for Stellar Events.'

He made a rude sound. 'A likely story.'

He put his hands on the other side of her tray and the glasses wobbled precariously. Zoe came out of her shock. 'Hey, watch it. I *am* actually working here.'

'I don't think so. Give me the tray and get out of here.'

Zoe glared at him. 'No, I'm just doing my job. You can't chuck me out every time you see me.'

She gave a tug of the tray at the same moment that he relaxed his grip and stumbled backwards under the weight of it, losing her balance. As if in slow motion she watched the tray tip up towards her and then the inevitable trajectory of about a dozen glasses, full of sparkling wine, falling towards her and then crashing to the artfully polished concrete floor, spraying wine in an arc around them.

A second afterwards there was a collective sharp intake of breath and then silence. Zoe stood in shock, the front of her shirt soaked. Wine had splashed up into her face.

She stared at Maks Marchetti. He looked grim. There was movement near them and Zoe's boss appeared in her eyeline. An officious man in a suit, he'd been stressed already, and now he looked ready to blow completely. His face was red.

Zoe held the tray to her chest like a shield. She started to say, 'Steven, I'm so sorry—

'Stop talking. Clean this up and then see me in the kitchen.'

He made a motion to another waiter Zoe didn't know and he rushed over with a brush and pan. Someone else arrived with paper towels.

Zoe couldn't look at Maks Marchetti again. She bent down and started picking up the bigger pieces of glass, sucking in a breath when she pierced her finger.

Suddenly Marchetti was beside her, taking her hand, looking at the blood. 'Leave the glass. You'll hurt yourself.'

Zoe pulled her hand back, shocked at the zing of electricity that raced up her arm. She glared at him. 'As if you care. Just leave me alone, will you? You've already caused enough trouble.'

She ignored the pain in her finger and continued to pick up the glass. When she stood again, her face burning with humiliation, Marchetti was gone.

She went back to the kitchen, where her boss was waiting for her. She put down the tray full of bits of broken glass and he handed her an envelope. His rage was icy, but his face was even redder now.

'Do you have any idea who that was?'

Zoe's stomach sank. This wasn't going to end well. 'Unfortunately, I do know who that was.'

'What on earth were you doing, tussling over a tray with him?' He waved a hand, as if he didn't even want to hear her answer, then said, 'Maks Marchetti is one of the most important people in the fashion and luxury industry. And not only that, but his brother Nikos is here too this evening.' He handed her an envelope. 'I'm sorry, Zoe, but we can't keep you on this evening—not after this. We won't be contacting you again.'

Zoe's mouth dropped open. She started to formulate her defence and stopped. Nothing she could say would reverse this. They wouldn't forgive her for this public humiliation.

Before he left, Steven glanced at her hand. 'You're dripping blood everywhere. Clean yourself up, please, and leave.' Then he swept out.

Zoe looked at her hand stupidly. At her cut finger. Numbly she searched for and found a first aid kit, and cleaned the cut and put a plaster on her finger, wincing as it throbbed. She welcomed the pain. Damn Maks Marchetti anyway. Now she *really* hoped she never saw him again.

But unfortunately that was not to be the case. When

she stepped into the street from the staff entrance a short while later, she saw a sleek low-slung silver car by the kerb. The door opened and a man uncoiled his tall, lean body from the driver's seat.

Maks Marchetti.

She started walking away, but he kept pace easily beside her. She was aware of her worn black trousers, white shirt—still damp from the wine—and her even more worn leather jacket. Flat shoes. Backpack on her back. She couldn't have been less like one of the women in that glittering space. And why did that even matter to her?

She stopped and rounded on Maks Marchetti. 'Look, what do you want now? I've been fired—isn't that enough for you? The last time I heard, streets were public spaces, so I don't think I'm actually infringing on hallowed Marchetti Group property now, am I?' She stopped, surprised at the depth of emotion she was feeling.

Maks put up a hand. To her surprise, he looked slightly...sheepish. He lowered his hand. 'I owe you an apology.'

Stupidly, Zoe said, 'You do?' And then she remembered what had happened. 'Yes, you do, actually.'

'I didn't mean for you to get fired. I saw you across the room and I...'

Maks trailed off, rendered uncharacteristically inarticulate for the first time in his life. He hadn't been able to get the woman in front of him out of his head for the past two weeks. She'd dominated his waking and sleeping moments.

When he'd spotted her across that room he'd been so surprised to see her that any kind of rationality had gone out of the window. He'd even forgotten that he'd come to the grudging conclusion that she wasn't actually paparazzi.

The truth was that she'd got to him. On some visceral level. From the moment he'd seen her camera lens pointed straight at him, provoking an extreme reaction. Not everyone would have reacted the way he had. His brother Nikos would have smiled and posed.

For Maks, though, camera lenses represented an intrusion of his privacy, and he'd spent the last two weeks wondering if he'd massively overreacted. A knee-jerk reaction to old trauma.

Yet when he'd seen her this evening, the mere sight of her had sparked that visceral reaction again. A need to see her up close juxtaposed with a need to push her away. And this time she hadn't even had a camera.

Because you took it.

Whatever it was about the way she made him react, he knew he couldn't let her walk away again. As much because he owed her this apology as for other, deeper and less coherent reasons.

Because you want her, whispered an inner voice.

He ignored it. She'd taken her hair down, but it couldn't hide her exquisite bone structure or delicate beauty. Or the scars. The one above her lip and the other one at her cheek. He wanted to reach out and trace them.

He curled his hand into a fist.

Abruptly he asked, 'Why did you sneak into the fashion show in Paris if it wasn't to take shots of celebrities and sell them?'

She swallowed. 'Do you believe I am not paparazzi?'

He nodded once. 'I looked through your photos. Street fashion shots. Landscapes. Architecture. People.'

Him. Zoe felt exposed again when she thought about focusing on his face that day two weeks ago.

His gaze lingered on her face now, intent. He looked at her scars. But, disconcertingly, like the last time, it didn't bother her as much as it had when she'd noticed people clocking them as they'd taken drinks from her tray at the event just now.

He was waiting for her response.

She sighed. 'I made an impulsive decision to sneak into the show when the opportunity presented itself. I've never been to a fashion show before, and they fascinate me. I was hoping that I might make some contacts with other photographers…break into the industry somehow. That's all.'

'You want to do fashion photography?'

Zoe squirmed a little. She'd never really articulated this to anyone before. 'It's something I've always been interested in, yes. But there's no way I'm remotely qualified.'

'Meanwhile you're working as a waitress?'

She shrugged self-consciously. 'Among other things—childminding, cleaning offices, teaching English to refugees… Although I'm not paid to do that.' She stopped talking, suddenly aware that she was babbling about her peripatetic career. And to Maks Marchetti, who must be one of the richest people on the planet.

Suddenly awkward, she stepped back. 'Thank you

for the apology. I'm sure you're required back inside. I should get going.' Zoe turned around.

'Wait.'

She stopped. Her heart was beating out of time. She felt breathless.

Maks Marchetti came and stood in front of her. To her surprise he said, 'Can we start again?' He held out a hand. 'I'm Maks Marchetti.'

Zoe knew she should just her head and step around him, saying something about having to get home and then put him out of her mind for good. But at that moment he smiled, and her breathlessness turned into asphyxiation. All good intentions turned to dust.

She had no defence for a smiling Maks Marchetti.

He'd been gorgeous from the moment she'd laid eyes on him, but he'd been aloof, and then condemnatory. Intimidating. She hadn't actually seen him smile. Not even when he'd been across the room at the event with that woman. But now he was smiling and he was…utterly irresistible.

Zoe had to force herself to breathe. She was feeling dizzy. And against every better judgement she found herself putting out her hand before she could stop herself. 'Zoe Collins. I'm Zoe Collins.'

Marchetti wrapped his hand around hers and that jolt of electricity zinged up her arm and into her blood. This time she didn't pull away. She couldn't.

He said, 'Zoe. It suits you. It's spiky.'

That gave Zoe the impetus to pull away. She almost cradled her hand to her body, as if she'd been burned. The air between them was charged. Zoe barely noticed people passing by. Traffic on the street. The warm early autumn evening. The dusky sky.

Her mouth tipped up ruefully. 'I'm not normally spiky. You seem to bring out the worst in me.'

Marchetti's smile faded. 'You lost your job because of me.'

Zoe made a face. 'It's not that big a deal, I only did a few jobs for them a month—if I was lucky.'

He looked at her for a long moment. And then he said, 'Still, I'd like to make it up to you. Will you join me for a drink?'

CHAPTER TWO

ZOE LOOKED AT him. 'A drink? Like…' She wanted to say *Like a date*, but stopped herself in time. The thought was too outlandish. Ridiculous. Maks Marchetti was feeling guilty, that was all.

He said, 'A drink. Like a way for me to apologise for being heavy-handed, not once but twice.'

See? Not a date.

As if she was anywhere close to his league, with her very ordinary looks and scars.

Zoe felt something drop inside her. He was being nice, that was all. 'Thank you—really. But you don't have to. It's fine. And I did trespass on your fashion show in Paris, so you were within your rights to throw me out.'

And confiscate my camera.

She felt a pang of pain when she thought of that.

Maks Marchetti said, 'It's not just to apologise, though. I'd like to take you for a drink to get to know you better. You…intrigue me.'

Zoe's brain seized. She intrigued him? Her, Zoe Collins, who wasn't remotely interesting. Not really.

'I…' She trailed off when she saw flashbulbs pop-ping behind him, where one of the A-list celebrities was leaving the venue. She gestured. 'Shouldn't you go back? Isn't that your event?'

Marchetti didn't even look. 'I've shown my face, seen who I needed to see.'

Zoe shook her head, fiercely trying to push down the excitement that had flared. *She intrigued him.*

'Mr Marchetti, that's your world and this is my world.' She gestured towards a nearby bus-stop. 'Thank you again for the offer, but it's probably not a good idea.'

Before she could take a step back he grimaced and said, 'It's Maks. *Mr Marchetti* reminds me of my father—never a good thing.'

Why? Zoe wanted to ask. But couldn't.

Then he frowned. 'Do you have a boyfriend at home?'

Zoe knew it would be the easiest lie and then she would be able to walk away, never to see him again. But something rogue inside her made her shake her head. 'No. I live alone. I am…alone.'

She hadn't meant it to come out like that, but as she said the words she felt a familiar sense of hollowness inside her. A chasm that she'd tried to fill with intimacy before, which had been a huge error of judgement.

She'd shied away from any kind of intimacy since. But the thought of walking away from Maks Marchetti right now was causing an almost physical resistance inside her. A little voice cajoled her. *It's just a drink— how dangerous could that be?* Except Zoe had a sense that, while she felt she could trust Maks Marchetti on a physical level, on an emotional level it would be a whole other story and one she hadn't really considered.

'So?' he asked. 'What's stopping you?'

It's just a drink.

Now Zoe felt ridiculous. She was projecting way too much onto what she was sure was just a polite overture, even if he had said she intrigued him.

'Okay, then. Yes, I'd like that.'

Maks wasn't prepared for the relief he felt. Most women he asked out were all too eager. Zoe had looked as if she was considering his question from a million angles before coming to her decision. Not what he was used to, but then he sensed nothing about this woman would be usual.

He said, 'I know a place not far from here. I'll drive.'

She looked at his car and seemed to go slightly pale in the dusky light, but then she said, 'Okay.'

Maks sent a quick text to give notice of their arrival, and as he drove he noticed that Zoe's hands were tight on the backpack on her lap.

'You're a nervous passenger?'

She flicked him a quick glance. 'Something like that.'

'You don't drive?'

She shook her head. 'No. Living in London, I don't really need to anyway.'

That was the platitude trotted out by most people who hadn't learned to drive and who lived in London, but Maks sensed there was something more to it.

'Don't worry,' he said. 'I'm an excellent driver.'

She flicked him another glance. When she saw his face she smiled and let out a small chuckle. 'I guess that shouldn't surprise me.'

Maks smiled back. He felt ridiculously buoyed up, to have defused her tension.

After a few minutes he pulled to a smooth stop outside an anonymous-looking townhouse. He unclipped his seatbelt as a valet came around to his door. 'This is a private club. I hope that's okay?'

Zoe did her best to sound nonchalant. 'Sure.'

Someone opened her door and she got out, her legs feeling slightly wobbly as they inevitably did after a car journey—even a short one. Maks hadn't lied, though. She'd felt cocooned in his car, and he'd driven with total confidence and competence.

For someone who was as hyper-alert as she was in cars, she'd almost let go of her alertness for a moment. A disconcerting sensation to admit to.

Maks joined her where she stood on the pavement. He indicated a set of steps that led up to a huge oak door. There were no markings on the building and Zoe sensed the exclusivity.

She moved forward and went up the steps, very aware of the man just behind her. As she got closer to the door she wondered why this moment should feel so momentous. She really didn't want it to. She didn't want to attribute anything special to this…date. She was sure it would be a one-off. And she told herself it wasn't as if she was in the market for anything more—not with her woeful track record…

The door opened and a sleek uniformed woman stood back to let them enter. 'Miss Collins and Mr Marchetti, you're very welcome. Shall I take your coats?'

Surprise that the hostess knew her name had Zoe

hesitating on the threshold for a second. Then Maks's hand touched her back. It was barely noticeable through two layers of clothes, yet it burned like a brand.

As Zoe followed Maks's barely discernible prompt to move forward into the hushed space, she knew with a sense of doom that she was in trouble. Because this felt momentous, and there was nothing she could do to quash it.

'What do you think?'

Maks looked at Zoe's rapt face as she took in the surroundings of the private club. She was looking up at a massive chandelier lit with hundreds of fake candles that flickered with a surprisingly realistic effect. He wanted to tuck her hair behind her ear so he could see her better. And then he wondered what the hell he was thinking. He never usually indulged in moments of PDA, even minute ones. They tended to be misconstrued.

Zoe said, 'It's…very decadent. It reminds me of a boudoir.' She glanced at him quickly. 'Not that I've ever been in a boudoir.'

Pink tinged her cheeks. He wondered if she kept her hair down to hide her scars.

He looked around and made a face. 'It's a bit over the top, and about five years out of date. We're redecorating soon.'

She looked at him. 'You own this place?'

'It's part of our portfolio,' he said carelessly.

'Is there anywhere you *don't* own?'

He looked at her. 'Plenty…but we're working on it.'

'Total world domination?'

He smiled minutely. 'Something like that.'

They looked at each other for a long moment and eventually she broke the contact. 'Why are there curtains on every booth?'

She was looking at the long heavy velvet curtains, currently drawn back from their own booth.

'So that they can be pulled across if one wants privacy.'

She frowned. 'But why—?'

And then she stopped suddenly, the pink in her cheek deepening as she obviously thought it through.

'Oh.'

Oh, indeed.

It was a long time since Maks had seen a woman blush and it had a direct effect on his blood. Making it surge. He shifted in the seat.

A waiter approached at that moment, with a tray containing a bottle of champagne in an ice bucket and two glasses. When the waiter had poured the champagne and left, Zoe said, 'Is this really necessary? This isn't a date.'

Maks handed her a glass and looked at her as he said, 'Isn't it?'

Zoe's heart palpitated. Maks was so close she could see that his eyes were lighter grey around the edges. His jaw was stubbled.

He tipped his glass towards hers. *'Salute.'*

After a moment she clinked her glass on his and it gave a melodic chime. 'Cheers.'

She took a sip of wine and it fizzed against her

tongue, igniting her taste buds, leaving a crisp, dry taste in her mouth.

'Your accent…you're not English?' he asked.

Zoe tensed. She wouldn't have expected him to notice that. He was foreign himself. She shook her head. 'No, I'm Irish. But I've been living here since I was eighteen.'

'Do you have family in Ireland?'

She shook her head quickly, instinctively shying away from more questions. She deflected the attention to him. 'You're Italian?'

'Half-Italian, half-Russian. My mother was Russian.'

'And you have…brothers?' Zoe knew he shared control of the Marchetti Group, but not much more than that.

He nodded. 'Two half-brothers. And one half-sister on my mother's side. She was the result of an affair my mother had with an American bodyguard. One of her many affairs while married to my father.'

This was said with no intonation of emotion, but Zoe sensed the undercurrents. 'Are you close to your brothers and sister?'

A muscle pulsed in Maks's jaw. 'My brothers and I didn't grow up together. It's only since our father died and we took control of the company that we've got to know one another better. So, no, I wouldn't say we're close, but I am very close to my sister.'

'How old is she?'

'Sasha is twenty-five.'

The same age as Zoe. It sounded as if his parents' marriage had been volatile, which would have undoubtedly brought him and his sister together.

Afraid that he would ask about her family again, Zoe asked, 'Did you spend time in Russia, growing up?'

He took a sip of champagne and shook his head. Zoe noticed his hands. Masculine. Long fingers. Strong. A shiver of something that felt like longing went through her.

'Not really. My mother's family cut ties with her when she married my father and he got his hands on her inheritance. It was his modus operandi—fleecing his wives of their fortunes to fund his own ambitions.'

She was surprised at his honesty.

As if reading her mind, he said sardonically, 'I'm not telling you anything that isn't available online.'

'So where *did* you grow up?'

'Rome and Paris, mainly.'

At that moment they were interrupted by a young woman in a trouser suit, hair tied back. She looked at Zoe. 'Sorry to interrupt,' she said. Then she looked at Maks as she handed him a small bag. 'This is it, sir.'

He took it. 'Thanks, Maria.'

The girl left and Maks handed the slightly bulky-looking bag to Zoe. 'This is yours.'

She took it and her heart thumped as she felt the weight and shape of it. She looked at Maks as she opened the cloth bag and took out her camera. The rush of relief was almost overwhelming. As was the surge of emotion.

When she'd gathered herself she looked at him. 'I thought you would have thrown it away.'

'I almost did…but something stopped me.'

'I'm glad you didn't.' Her voice was husky.

'It's important to you. Clearly.'

She nodded. 'It belonged to my father. He was a photographer…among other things.'

'Would I have heard of him?'

Zoe avoided answering directly by saying, 'He died a long time ago—that's why this camera has such sentimental value for me.'

'You're a good photographer. Did you study?'

She shook her head, self-conscious now. 'I'm self-taught.'

'So you sneaked into that show to try and get some experience.'

Shame lanced her. She put the camera down. 'Look, I'm so sorry—'

But he cut her off, saying gruffly, 'When I saw your camera pointing at me I overreacted. I don't tolerate invasions of privacy well. My sister and I…we were constantly hounded by the paparazzi while we were growing up, thanks to our parents' very public affairs, fights and then divorce.'

'I'm sorry to hear that.'

Maks shrugged. 'It came with the territory.'

'How old were you when they divorced?'

'About fifteen. My mother is on husband number three now.'

Maks's voice was hard and flat, brooking no further discussion. She could empathise with that. There was a lot she didn't want to talk about either.

She picked up the camera again. 'Thank you for this. It means a lot.'

'Why did you take a photograph of me?'

Zoe felt heat rise into her face. She forced herself to look at Maks, even though she was squirming inside. She felt defensive under that cool grey gaze. 'I'm sure you don't need me to tell you you're a good-looking man.'

'There were infinitely better-looking men than me there that day.'

Zoe could have debated that point. She shrugged, trying to feign a nonchalance she wasn't feeling. 'You caught my eye… Everyone else was looking around, looking for attention, but you looked…contained.' Zoe winced. How could she articulate the way he'd sent off such an aloof vibe…?

Maks's mouth twitched. 'I don't tolerate small-talk well. Inane conversation, talk of the latest trends… I like to make my own judgements.'

His gaze narrowed on her and Zoe felt breathless all over again. A hazard with this man.

He said, '*You* caught my attention.'

Her heart thumped. 'But… I'm nothing special.'

Maks knew she wasn't fishing for compliments. She sounded genuinely perplexed.

'I haven't stopped thinking about you for the past two weeks. I kept your camera. I looked through your photographs. There are none of you.'

'Why would I take pictures of myself?'

'You're beautiful.'

Her expression shut down, and she avoided his eye. 'You don't have to say things like that. I know I'm not.'

Once again Maks fought the urge to tip up her chin, make her look at him. 'You might not be seven feet tall and have the kind of outlandish traffic-stopping looks that models have, but, yes, you're beautiful.'

* * *

Zoe glanced at Maks suspiciously. But he wasn't laughing at her. She'd been given compliments before, and she'd found herself soaking them up like a flower responding to the sun's rays, but soon she'd realised they were empty compliments, used to manipulate her.

This felt different. Which made it dangerous. Because she'd extricated herself from a situation with an ex-boyfriend who had been infinitely less in every way than the man in front of her.

Maks Marchetti left Dean Simpson in the dust. So how much more damage could a man like Maks do, if she left him in?

She didn't want to answer that, because on the other side of fear was something she didn't want to acknowledge: *hope*. She'd allowed herself to feel hope before and had learnt a harsh lesson. Did she really want to risk that again?

No.

'Look, I'm under no illusions. Your industry celebrates perfect beauty, and we both know that I do not come close to that ideal. Not with a scarred face.'

Maks cocked his head to one side, looking at her. His gaze moved over her face and she felt hot again. She cursed herself for drawing his attention like this. She'd hoped mention of her scars, of the fact that she wasn't perfect, might act as a deterrent. Remind him that she only intrigued him. Nothing more.

'Perfection is overrated. Believe me. I'm far more interested in beautiful flaws. Everyone is flawed, Zoe, but most just hide it underneath a pseudo-perfect exterior.'

Zoe's breath hitched. She really hadn't expected to

hear him say something like that. His words resonated deep inside her, where she held exactly the same sentiments.

Before she could respond, Maks was reaching for her hand and holding it up. Electricity short-circuited her brain.

He was frowning. 'Your finger—is it okay?'

She looked at her hand stupidly and saw the plaster over her injured finger. She wasn't sure if it was throbbing now because of him or because it hurt. She couldn't pull her hand back.

'It's fine. It wasn't a deep cut.'

'Still, it was my fault you hurt yourself.'

Zoe forced herself to move her hand away. 'Honestly, it's fine.'

She took another sip of champagne, hoping it might calm the hectic beat of her pulse. She would never have expected someone like Maks Marchetti to prove to be so…perceptive. And the fact that he'd kept her camera and returned it kept emotion bubbling far too near the surface.

She needed to take a breath. Get her bearings before she lost all sense of reality. Before he could speak again or, worse, touch her and scramble her brain.

'Would you excuse me for a minute?' she asked.

Maks said, 'Of course.'

He motioned to one of the staff, who came over and showed Zoe where the restrooms were. She went inside and leant against the closed door for a moment, wondering if it would ever be possible to be in this man's company and not feel dizzy.

She chastised herself as she pushed away from the

door. She wouldn't be seeing him again. Stupid even to go there.

She went over to the sink and ran the cold tap, putting her wrists underneath the water and then splashing some on her face. She stood up and looked at herself critically. Her face was flushed, her eyes far too wide and awed-looking. Her hair was down and tousled—and not in a good way.

Her leather jacket looked worn, and her shirt still showed a damp stain from the spilled wine. Zoe groaned. She most definitely was not sophisticated—or beautiful. Especially not when compared to the women she'd been serving wine to at the event. The man needed his eyes checked. Perhaps he only found her interesting because she was so different to everyone else in his milieu? He was just jaded.

She battled against the fizz in her blood that spoke of too many dangerous things—excitement chief among them.

She couldn't indulge this heady moment any longer.

Maks watched Zoe return to the table. The lines of her body were tense and her eyes were avoiding his. He knew instinctively even before she opened her mouth what she was going to say.

She stopped at the other side of the table and finally looked at him. 'This has been lovely. Thank you for the drink, but I really should be going now. I have to work in the morning and I don't live near here.'

Maks had to curb every urge he had to persuade her to stay. Not something he was used to having to do. She reminded him of a fawn, ready to bolt. She was resisting this…this thing between them, and he was more intrigued than ever.

He said, with a carelessness he didn't feel, 'Sure, no problem. I'll give you a lift home.'

Her eyes grew wide. 'Really, there's no need, I'm all the way over in East London. It'll be far quicker on the Tube.'

Maks looked at his watch. It was after eleven p.m. 'And more dangerous,' he said. 'I insist. The roads will be quiet now. It won't take any longer.'

She looked as if she was inclined to argue, but eventually said, 'Okay—if you're sure it's not out of your way.'

It was. Massively. But for the first time in a long time Maks felt energised, and there was no way he was letting this woman slip through his fingers again.

'It's not a problem.'

He stood up and led the way out. The hostess behaved with utter discretion and showed no hint of surprise even though they'd only arrived a short while before.

Back in the car, Zoe gave him directions and Maks drove away from the Bond Street area. He could see her hands clasping her bag again out of the corner of his eye. She was tense.

To distract her, he asked, 'Why did you leave Ireland? By all accounts the country is thriving. My brother has a house there and his wife is Irish. They have a baby son.'

Just saying those words sent a fresh jolt of shock through Maks. He was still coming to terms with the fact that his playboy brother Nikos had recently discovered that he'd fathered a child and was now married.

The thought of being careless enough to find himself having to consider marriage for the sake of a child made Maks go cold. No way would he subject any child of his to the prospect of a dysfunctional marriage, and he didn't know any other kind.

Beside him, Zoe shrugged. He welcomed a diversion from thoughts of his brother and babies and marriage.

'I wanted to travel and explore the world outside of Ireland.'

'Have you been anywhere else?' Maks glanced at her and saw that her hair had swung forward again. He had to stop himself from pulling it back. He hated not being able to see her face.

'A little...around Europe. Not as much as I'd like.'

Maks, having become used to reading people and situations ever since his parents had waged their psychological warfare, guessed that Zoe wasn't giving him the whole story. But he wouldn't push. For now.

A companionable silence fell in the sleek car as it easily ate up the distance between the fashionable centre of London and the far less salubrious area where she lived. Zoe hated to admit how comfortable she felt. She wasn't used to comfortable silences with men. Although admittedly she didn't have much experience...

'It's the next right and then immediately left,' Zoe said quickly, realising they were practically at her door. 'This is fine.'

Maks pulled to a smooth stop in a space between two cars. 'You live here?'

Zoe bristled slightly, imagining how the tall, scruffy house must look to him. 'Yes. My flat is on the top floor.' *Her tiny, one-bedroom flat.*

Maks undid his belt and opened his door, getting out. Zoe had to scramble to catch up. He was already at the bottom of her steps.

He put out a hand. 'Your keys?'

Zoe looked at him. 'I can let myself in. This is fine—you can go now.'

He shook his head. 'I'm not leaving until I know you're safe.'

She let out an exasperated sound. 'This area is probably safer than where we just were! It's a tight-knit community.'

'Zoe.'

She shivered at the way he said her name, with a slight hint of an accent, an emphasis on the *'Z'*, making it sound exotic, and at his insistence on seeing her safe.

His hair glinted under the moonlight and he looked almost otherworldly against the very humdrum backdrop of houses. Yet he wasn't getting out of there as quickly as he could. Rushing back to his rarefied world.

She dug into her bag and held out her keys, saying a little huffily, 'You're being ridiculous.'

He took the keys and went up the steps. She followed him. He opened the front door, which didn't stick the way it usually did for her. Then, instead of giving her the keys, he said, 'Lead on.'

Zoe rolled her eyes. 'You asked for it—there are five flights and no lift.'

But of course who was out of breath when they got to the top? Not Maks, who was showing no signs of strain.

Zoe could feel the heat in her cheeks and beads of sweat on her brow, the lack of breath. Except she couldn't be sure if that was from the exertion or knowing he had been right behind her the whole way up.

She turned around at her door and held out her hand. 'My keys, please. I'm safe now.'

Maks held on to her keys. 'How do you know there isn't an intruder inside?'

Zoe wanted to stamp her foot. 'I'm sure there isn't.'

Maks arched his brow. 'You're really not even going to offer me some water before I make the long trip back down to the bottom?'

There was a glint of devilry in his eyes that completely dissolved Zoe's resistance. She grabbed the keys out of his hand. 'Fine—you can assure yourself that I'm totally safe.'

She turned around and opened the door and pushed it open, turning on the light at the same time. The soft glow illuminated the tiny room, with its sofa covered in a colourful throw and the plants by the window, which was open a crack to let air in. Photos covered every available wall space.

Zoe turned around, expecting to see horror on Maks's face at such a rustic basic room, but he was stepping over the threshold, his eyes taking it all in, not looking surprised. Looking...interested.

At the last moment Zoe remembered her manners. 'I don't have anything alcoholic, but I can offer you some tea or coffee?'

'Coffee would be great, thank you. Black, no sugar.'

No frills. Like the man.

Zoe went into her tiny galley kitchen, off which was

the even smaller bedroom and bathroom. She made the coffee, glancing through the hatch to see what Maks was up to. His hands were in his pockets and he was staring at the photos on the wall.

The fact that he was here, in her private space, should feel…overwhelming. She'd never felt entirely comfortable when Dean had been here, which should have been an alarm she paid heed to. But Maks being here…it didn't feel intrusive, or uncomfortable. She felt safe.

She brought him his coffee and he took the cup, barely glancing at her. 'Who is this?' He pointed to a black and white picture on the wall. It was of a young girl with a huge smile that almost eclipsed the horrific scars on her face.

Zoe held her own mug of coffee in both hands. 'That's Fatima. She's a refugee from Syria. I do some work with the Face Forward charity.'

Maks looked at her. He was frowning. 'That was set up by Ciro Sant'Angelo, no? To help people with scarring?'

Zoe nodded, feeling self-conscious of her own scars. 'Do you know him?'

Ciro Sant'Angelo was an Italian billionaire—she wouldn't be surprised.

Maks looked back at the picture. 'Our paths have crossed. I admire what he's doing. This is a great photo.'

'Thank you.' Zoe felt ridiculously pleased at his praise.

He looked at her. 'If it's not too personal a question, how did you get your scars?'

Zoe had no time to school her expression or hide. She'd absently tucked her hair behind her ears. So she couldn't escape Maks's intense gaze, demanding the full truth. Behind him, on a shelf, she could see the framed photograph of herself and her family, taken before that awful—

A lump rose in her throat and she spoke quickly to counteract it. 'It was a car accident.'

'Is that how your father died?'

Zoe nodded quickly, pushing down the emotion. 'And my mother and little brother.'

Maks frowned. 'How old were you?'

'Eight.' Her voice was clipped. Abrupt.

'That's why you were tense in the car? Why you don't drive?'

She nodded.

There was a silence. And then, 'Zoe... I—'

She cut him off, dreading his pity. 'It's fine. You don't have to say anything. It was a long time ago. It was an accident.'

My fault.

Feeling far too exposed now, on a million levels, Zoe took the coffee cup out of Maks's hand and took it back to the kitchen, not caring that she was slopping coffee on her floor.

'Like I said, I have to work tomorrow.'

She came back into the living area and went to the front door, opening it. She avoided looking directly at Maks, which wasn't the easiest thing when he took up so much space.

'Thank you for dropping me home.'

'I take it you're asking me to leave?'

His tone was dry. She glanced at him, suddenly afraid that he wouldn't take no for an answer, even though instinctively she felt safe with him, which was something she didn't really want to analyse.

But he didn't look angry. He appeared unconcerned that she was being so rude. She felt contrite. 'Yes, look…sorry. It's been a long day.'

So why didn't she feel tired? Why did she feel as if she was full of fizzing anticipation and a breathlessness that was becoming far too familiar in his presence?

Maks looked at Zoe. She was tense again. Reminding him of that fawn, ready to bolt.

He walked towards her and saw how her hand tightened on the door handle.

'Okay, I can take a hint. I'll leave… But before I do I want you to be honest with me.'

She looked up at him and Maks had to stop himself from staring at her soft mouth.

'What do you mean?'

'You feel it too, don't you? This…energy between us. Chemistry. Desire.'

Colour spilled into her cheeks even as she shook her head. When she spoke she sounded breathless, and it had a direct effect on Maks's body.

'No, I don't… I don't think I do.'

Maks smiled, because it was a long time since he'd had to seduce a woman. 'Liar.'

Now Zoe looked bewildered. 'Why are you interested in me?'

'Why are you so suspicious?'

'Because I'm just…nothing special. And I'm not looking for compliments.'

'I know,' Maks said.

'I'm just normal. Nothing extraordinary.'

'Your pictures aren't *"just normal"*. You have a talent. And you're beautiful. I want you, Zoe, more than I've wanted anyone in a long time.'

Her cheeks glowed. 'You're very direct. Has anyone ever told you that?'

A memory flashed into Maks's head of his mother, her face contorted with fury, her hand coming out of nowhere to slap him across the cheek, her spittle hitting his face as she said, *'I owe you nothing.'*

'On a rare occasion,' Maks said dryly, pushing down that rogue memory of the time when he'd confronted his mother about her woeful mothering skills.

Zoe looked up at Maks Marchetti. She couldn't believe he'd just told her he wanted her. *Her.* Boring, ordinary Zoe Collins.

But he didn't think she was ordinary, or boring.

It was too seductive…too much. She could feel secret parts of herself that she'd exposed before wanting to unfurl and bask in this man's dynamic presence. *Dangerous* to want those things. Because she'd wanted them before and she'd paid for it. For her naivety. For her vulnerability.

But, in truth, Dean Simpson hadn't really had the power to truly wound her. She'd had a lucky escape. Whereas this man… She sensed a level of danger that she would be wise to heed.

He looked as immovable as a massive stone statue. But treacherously, in the same moment she could acknowledge the danger, she also felt it dissipating, to be replaced by temptation.

Desperation gripped her at the thought that he might see how tempted she was. She needed to nip this in the bud now—prove to Maks that he was delusional. Surely if she could prove that he'd leave, and then she could get on with her life and forget that she'd ever met him?

As if you could forget a man like this, taunted an inner voice.

It was a taunt that turned her desperation to panic. Panic strong enough to make her step closer to him and say, 'I'll prove to you that there's really nothing between us.'

A glint came into his eye. 'Go on, then.'

CHAPTER THREE

ZOE KNEW HE was issuing a challenge, but she had no option but to follow it through now. She sucked in a breath and stepped even closer. Maks made no move to touch her. She reached up, putting her hands on his shoulders, coming up on her toes.

He was so tall, so broad. Every part of her tingled with her awareness of him as a virile male in his prime.

That had to be all it was. She was only human. It couldn't be desire uniquely for *him*. And he would soon realise that she really didn't hold any appeal for him.

She reached up as much as she could, her hands gripping his shoulders, and pressed her mouth to his before she could lose her nerve.

But the nerves, the sense of panic, the desire to prove him wrong…all was incinerated in a flash of electric heat as soon as her lips met the firm contours of his mouth.

Zoe was vaguely aware that she'd intended this to be a quick physical transaction, merely to prove Maks Marchetti wrong. But she couldn't move. *Didn't want to.* Her lips clung to his in a timeless moment when everything was suspended on a breath…which she finally let out like a sigh against his mouth.

It was a sigh of resignation, a sigh of futility, a sigh of recognition that the hectic throbbing pulse of her blood wasn't just because she was a human reacting to a virile male. It was because something in her resonated so deeply with something in him that she would never be the same again.

She could feel the sheer whipcord strength of his body but she was still not close enough. She wanted to move against him, let all that heat and strength envelop her.

Of their own volition her lips opened, as if they literally couldn't bear to keep shut. Breath flowed. Her tongue-tip moved forward, seeking to taste. But she had barely touched the seam of his mouth when she suddenly realised what she was doing and pulled back, as if stung.

Maks Marchetti was looking at her. She realised that she was still clinging to him, reaching up, straining to get closer. She pulled her hands off him and stepped back so suddenly she almost fell.

Her cheeks burned. She ducked her head and let her hair fall around her face. She was terrified to look at him again and see his expression. Terrified to get confirmation of what she'd set out to prove—that he couldn't possibly want her.

She'd failed miserably in proving she didn't want him, though. She'd been clinging to him like a monkey, and she was sure he'd only been seconds away from having to physically remove her—

'Zoe… I can practically hear your thoughts, they're so loud.'

She looked up before she could stop herself. His eyes

were glittering, almost silver now. His mouth was quirking. This was even worse. He was *laughing* at her.

Zoe stalked over to the door and pulled it open. She didn't look at him again. 'I think you should leave now.'

He came over and the door was pushed closed again. But Maks was still in the room. Zoe looked at him. He was shaking his head. No quirking mouth now. Deadly serious.

He reached out and tucked a lock of her hair behind her ear. And then he moved closer. The air grew thick and heavy. His hand was still in her hair.

He said, 'May I?'

Zoe's heart beat fast. He hadn't left. He wasn't laughing at her. He was looking at her mouth as if mesmerised and now…at her eyes. She had nowhere to hide. She just nodded.

He made a total mockery of her clumsy kiss by taking her face in his hands and tilting it up to his with an assurance born of experience and mastery. She could feel the rough abrasion of his palms and fingers against her jaw and cheeks. Rough, not smooth. Evidence that he wasn't as civilised as he looked.

His mouth touched hers, lightly at first, as if testing… Zoe held her breath, afraid to move in case he stopped. Their breaths intermingled. He kissed the corner of her mouth, taking her by surprise. And then the other corner, where the scar dissected her lip.

Her legs felt weak. She had to lock her knees to stay standing.

And then his mouth settled over hers completely, and she had to close her eyes against the burning intensity in his for fear that he might see the effect he was having on her.

His mouth was hard, but soft, coaxing a response that she couldn't hold back, giving it as instinctively as a flower gave itself to the power of the sun. She opened her mouth on a sigh that turned into a shiver of excitement when Maks's tongue touched hers, demanding more, demanding everything.

Zoe had been kissed before. She'd even enjoyed it—until she hadn't. But this went beyond mere enjoyment. This was…elemental. A conflagration burning her up from the inside out, leaving no cell untouched or unscorched.

Time faded away. All she was aware of was the hectic beat of her heart and the pounding of her blood. She strained to get closer to Maks, winding her arms around his neck.

And then he broke the kiss.

Zoe opened her eyes with effort. She was dizzy. She realised she was all but plastered to Maks and that his hands were on her waist, helping to support her.

Her breath was choppy. Shakily she took her arms down and moved aside, dislodging Maks's hands.

'I think that's proved the point,' he said.

Her brain felt sluggish. She felt undone. 'The point…'

'That there's chemistry between us.'

Was that what it was called?

Zoe's whole body was throbbing. She wanted Maks to kiss her again, to stop talking. She knew she didn't want to think about what was happening here, because that would be way too scary.

He took a step back. Her belly lurched. 'Where are you going?'

'You want me to stay?'

'I—'

She stopped. For a moment she'd almost said *yes*, and as the full realisation of that sank in—how quickly she'd forgotten what had happened the last time she'd allowed a man close—sanity cooled her heated brain.

'No, I don't want you to stay.'

'Even if you said yes, I'd still leave.'

Zoe looked at him. She was surprised, and not liking the little voice that whispered inside her head. *He's different. This is different.*

'Why?'

Maks took a step closer again. 'Because I can see that you're not ready. You're skittish. Something has happened to you. You don't trust me.'

It took a few seconds for Zoe to absorb that, and when she did his words landed in her belly like a cold stone. *'Something has happened to you. You don't trust me.'* She felt totally exposed now. In a way that she'd promised herself she wouldn't ever again.

Zoe folded her arms. 'You think you see a lot, Mr Marchetti.'

He smiled, but it was rueful. 'I'm good at reading people. A lesson I learnt at the hands of selfish and self-absorbed parents.'

She didn't want to know that about him. She didn't want to think of him and his sister dealing with their parents' bitter divorce.

She went to the door and opened it.

Maks said from behind her, 'Give me your phone.'

She turned around. 'Why would I do that?'

'Because this doesn't end here. But I'm going to leave the ball in your court.'

Torn between wanting to shut down that arrogance and wanting to know what he meant to do, Zoe made a huffing sound and then went to her backpack and pulled out her phone. She handed it to Maks, who took it and punched in some numbers. He handed it back, and somehow she resisted the urge to check it. There was something about his confidence that was as irritating as it was seductive.

He went to the door. She felt that lurch again—as if something very primal inside her objected to him leaving.

She walked over. He was already on the other side of the door.

'I look forward to hearing from you,' he said.

Zoe held on to the door. 'You might not hear from me at all.'

He looked at her for a long moment. 'I think I will. And then you'll tell me what happened to you.'

The thought of telling him of her humiliation made her go cold. It helped her to stiffen her spine and say, 'Goodbye, Maks.'

He shook his head as he backed away, his mouth quirking up. '*Ciao,* Zoe.'

He turned, and he'd disappeared down the stairs before she could say anything else. She closed the door only after she'd heard the door close downstairs, and then the powerful throttle of his car's engine.

She got ready for bed in a bit of a stupor, still slightly stunned at everything that had happened this evening.

She'd lost her job.

In fairness, it hadn't exactly been her main source of income. Truth be told, she didn't have a main source of income. She was an expert in doing lots of things and committing to none. Not even photography. Because committing to something meant showing some kind of vulnerability, risking a massive fail or, worse, pain and loss.

Zoe scowled at herself in the small bathroom mirror. And that was why she didn't need to invite a man like Maks Marchetti into her life. Because he saw too much and he made her feel too much. And not just physically. That impulse she'd had to ask him to stay scared her even now. It had been so immediate. Visceral. And he was a stranger.

But you want him in a way that's different—

She clamped down on painful memories. She'd confused desire with being able to trust someone before. But that kiss had blown any kind of understanding of desire she'd had before out of the water. What she'd experienced had been child's play. This was the real deal. Earthy, raw, out of control. She knew instinctively that Maks Marchetti was a man who would demand nothing less than total surrender. And that was something Zoe couldn't imagine giving. To anyone. It would ask too much of her.

She looked at herself critically. Pyjamas buttoned up to the neck. Face scrubbed so clean that her scars stood out in pink lines. Superficial scars that hid far deeper scars.

Maks Marchetti would soon forget all about a woman who had intrigued him just for a moment. She wouldn't be using his number and he wouldn't be knocking on her door again.

* * *

'What?' Maks growled at his assistant without turning around from where he stood at the window of his London office.

The city was spread out before him, with the Thames snaking between iconic buildings and under even more iconic bridges, but Maks couldn't have cared less.

All that had consumed him for a week now was, *Why the hell hasn't she got in touch with me?*

Zoe Collins. The woman he'd shared probably the most chaste kiss of his life with, and yet it had left an erotic imprint that lingered in his blood, waking him every night with his body aching for sexual fulfilment.

'Um…boss, it's the fact that you're meant to be overseeing that shoot in New York at the moment…'

Maks turned around to face the young man. He arched a brow. 'And clearly I'm not?'

Because he was loath to leave London in case she called. When he never normally made decisions based on a lover who wasn't even a lover. *Yet.* The thought that she might never be a lover evoked an almost violent reaction inside him.

He would know her.

'They've decided to reschedule and relocate to St Petersburg, in the hope that you can attend while you're there for your meetings.'

Maks should feel slightly chastened by the fact that one of the world's biggest fashion houses cared enough about his opinion to reschedule an advertising campaign to suit his schedule, but he didn't. He was filled with a sense of resolve.

'Tell them I'll be there.'

And I won't be alone.

No matter how he had to do it, he would have Zoe Collins by his side and in his bed.

Zoe packed her bag as the people left the classroom. One of the young women turned around at the door and came back, surprising Zoe with an impromptu hug.

Zoe hugged her back, and smiled. 'What's that for?'

'Just to say thank you. You don't know how much it means, you helping us find our way in this new life.'

Zoe blushed, embarrassed. 'Don't be daft. If I wasn't here someone else would be.'

The girl shook her head. She was serious. Too serious. She'd seen awful things. She'd lost her entire family.

'Maybe, Miss Collins. But you are the one here, helping us, so thank you.'

Zoe's heart constricted as she watched the young woman in the headscarf walk out. She couldn't imagine not being here to help these people. Teaching English to newly arrived immigrants was such a basic thing, and the sense of reward she got from it made her feel guilty enough that she was happy it was on a voluntary basis.

She was about to leave when her mobile phone pinged with a message. She frowned and picked it out of her bag. Not having close family or friends meant that she wasn't used to receiving the casual messages everyone else took for granted.

She unlocked her phone to see a text from...

Her heart stopped. *Him.*

Hi Zoe...

She texted back,

How do you have my number?

I made sure I called myself from your phone when I put in my number, so I knew I'd have it.

Zoe's heart was palpitating. All week he'd haunted her waking and sleeping moments. A dozen times she'd almost deleted his number and then stopped herself at the last moment.

She typed back.

I would have called you if I was interested.

An answer came almost immediately.

Oh, you're interested.

Zoe wanted to scowl, but it turned into a grudging smile. She couldn't deny the rush of excitement. And also a treacherous sense of relief.

Before she could think of how to respond to that he sent another text.

I'm outside, waiting for you. Interesting place.

Zoe nearly dropped her phone. She looked up, suddenly terrified he'd be lounging in the doorway, smirking at her. But it was empty. He could hardly mean...

She walked out of the room with her bag, down the corridor of the local community centre. Not the prettiest building in the world, by any stretch of the imagination, and certainly not the kind of place for a man like—

He was here.

Zoe stepped outside the main doors to see Maks Marchetti, lounging against the same low-slung car he'd been driving a week ago. Except this time he was dressed more casually, wearing dark trousers and a dark grey long-sleeved top. She didn't have to inspect it to guess that it was probably cashmere, and it clung to his muscles far too lovingly, leaving little to the imagination.

Zoe felt self-conscious in her worn jeans and T-shirt, worn under an even more worn V-necked jumper. Scuffed trainers.

She walked over. 'What are you doing here?' She sounded accusing and winced inwardly. This man precipitated extreme reactions in her.

'I got bored waiting for you to call and sought you out. You'd mentioned teaching English, and it wasn't hard to find out where some local classes were listed.'

Zoe hated to admit that she was impressed. 'You could have just called me.'

He shrugged. 'It wouldn't have been as much fun.'

She looked around the very ordinary car park in disbelief. 'As much fun as visiting East London again? You need to get out more.'

Maks chuckled. 'Perhaps I do.'

He stood up straight, reminding Zoe how tall he was. How powerful. How that mouth had felt on hers. Hot. A wave of desire made her legs feel momentarily weak.

'I've been invited to the opening of a photography

exhibition this evening. I thought you might like to come with me.'

Zoe hadn't expected him to say that. Curiosity got the better of her. 'What exhibition?'

'Taylor Cartwright's latest work.'

Zoe sucked in a breath at this mention of one of America's foremost landscape photographers, who had died recently, and said, almost to herself, 'It's been sold out for months…'

'Would you like to come?'

She was torn between jumping at the opportunity and her wariness at the thought of spending more time with a man who made her skin prickle with heat and a million other disturbing things.

Zoe looked at him suspiciously. 'And after the exhibition? Then what?'

'That's up to you. I'd like to take you for dinner, maybe a drink, or I can drop you home.'

Remembering that kiss, Zoe said quickly, 'I can make my own way home.'

'Whatever you wish.'

Maks looked at the woman in front of him. If his blood hadn't been humming just from being near her again he might have wondered why she had such a unique effect on him, but he wasn't capable of wondering about anything right now. He felt as if he'd scored a victory merely because she hadn't said no, and because she hadn't ruled out dinner or a drink.

The fact that he hadn't had to work so hard to seduce a woman *ever* was also not something he cared to think about right now.

Zoe couldn't have been less dressed to impress, but all he could see were those huge aquamarine eyes. Her hair was down, which he was guessing was her default, so she could hide behind it if she wanted to. It made him want to pull it back, so he could see her face more clearly. He barely noticed her scars. He was more distracted by her soft lips, and the erotic memory of how they'd opened under his mouth, the taste of her…

He cursed silently when his body responded.

'Okay. I'd like to come, thank you.'

Maks almost didn't hear her, he was trying so hard to get his body under control. 'Good. That's…good.'

Zoe made a face, and she suddenly looked shy. 'Would you mind if I stopped by my flat to change, though? Just for five minutes.'

Maks shook his head. 'Of course not. Let's go.'

A couple of hours later he was wondering why he'd been surprised when Zoe literally had only been in her flat for five minutes before re-emerging.

He looked at her across the gallery.

She'd changed into figure-hugging leather trousers and a soft V-necked cream sweater, under a dark grey jacket. Clothes designed not to draw attention. To blend in. Like the way she used that fall of honey-blonde hair to hide her face—most of the time.

She had a tomboyish style that made him want to see her dressed in long falls of silk and satin that would cling to her body and reveal those slender curves. That pale skin.

She was staring intently at a large photograph of Yosemite, the national park in America. His mouth thinned. Another first—a woman who wasn't utterly absorbed with him. Either feigning it or otherwise.

As if reading his mind, the woman beside him said, 'I like her already. She's not clinging to your arm as if she can't walk by herself or simpering about the latest nail varnish colours.'

Maks looked at his sister and said dryly, 'Sash, if I wasn't so emotionally barren you could really hurt me sometimes.'

His sister snorted derisively but Maks ignored her. It had been a bad idea to ask her to come. She was too astute for her own good.

Zoe knew she couldn't keep pretending that the photos held more fascination for her than the man she could see behind her through the crowd, reflected in the glass over the black and white image.

He was talking to a woman. Tall, slim. A dart of something hit Zoe in the solar plexus. A jolt of possessiveness. Which was ridiculous. They'd kissed once! He was obviously only interested because she wasn't falling into his arms like an overripe plum.

Steeling herself, Zoe turned around and walked back over towards Maks, whose dark grey gaze was unnervingly intent on her.

She took in the woman beside him. Something about her was familiar, but she knew she'd never seen her before. She was wearing nondescript clothes, a shirt and long skirt, as if she was trying to hide. Long hair... dark blonde. And she wore glasses. But Zoe realised that woman was extraordinarily beautiful. She was just trying to hide it.

Something about that resonated inside Zoe. The sense of a kindred spirit.

Maks gestured to the woman. 'Zoe, I'd like you to meet my sister, Sasha.'

His sister. A knot unclenched inside Zoe.

She put out her hand, smiled. 'Nice to meet you.'

Sasha shook her hand, smiled, and Zoe was nearly bowled backwards. She wasn't just beautiful. She was stunning.

'You too,' she said. 'I was just telling my darling brother—'

'Sash, didn't you say you had someone to meet?'

His sister's grey eyes danced mischievously. 'No… but I can take a hint. I hope we meet again, Zoe.'

Zoe watched her walk away, fading into the crowd. She turned to Maks. 'You didn't have to send her away.'

Maks took her arm. 'Oh, yes, I did. She was bound to embarrass me—it's her life's mission.'

Zoe's heart clenched. She'd had a younger brother. He would have been twenty-three. Would he have ribbed her like Sasha did Maks? Her heart ached.

Maks was looking down at her. 'Ready to go?'

Zoe nodded quickly, afraid he'd see the sudden melancholy in her eyes. She worked so hard not to think of those things. 'Thank you for this. I enjoyed seeing the photos.'

She didn't mention that Taylor Cartwright had been a mentor of her father's when he'd been young, travelling around North America and taking his first photographs.

Maks led her out of the gallery onto the street. Summer was tipping into autumn and there was the faintest chill in the evening air, a sign of things to come.

Zoe shivered slightly. Immediately Maks said, 'Are you cold?'

His solicitude melted the cold around her heart. She shook her head. 'No, I'm fine.'

'So, can I take you for dinner? There's a place not far from here.'

Seeing Maks with his sister and touching on the past again had made Zoe feel vulnerable. She didn't want to be alone. But she knew that was just an excuse.

She looked up at Maks. 'Sure, I'd like that.'

He smiled and, like his sister, it transformed his face, turning him from gorgeous into devastating.

He took her hand and led her to his car. She found that her usual anxiety around being in a car didn't surface when she was with him. He drove so competently, not trying to show off. He didn't need to. He oozed confidence.

Within ten minutes, Maks was driving down a quiet mews street.

Zoe frowned. 'Where are we?'

'Mayfair.'

He pulled to a stop outside one of the houses. It had dark brick and black-framed windows. It looked discreet and exclusive. She wondered if this was another private club.

As if reading her mind, Maks said, 'This is my London townhouse.'

Zoe looked at him. She opened her mouth, but then she realised that he hadn't actually specified where he was bringing her. He'd just said, *'There's a place...'*

'That's rather underhand of you.'

'I promise my intentions are very honourable. If you

feel uncomfortable in any way, I'll take you wherever you want to go.' He made a crossing his heart motion.

Zoe didn't trust him for a second. But it was more that she didn't trust herself, if she was totally honest. She unclicked her seatbelt and watched as Maks uncoiled his tall frame from the driver's seat to come round and help her out.

She was more intrigued than she liked to admit to see where he lived.

The door opened as Maks approached as if by magic. A middle-aged Asian man dressed in dark trousers and dark long-sleeved top greeted Maks.

'Hamish, I'd like you to meet Zoe Collins.'

The man stepped forward at the door, smiling and holding out his hand. 'You're probably wondering how I came by a name like Hamish? I was born and brought up in Scotland when my parents emigrated there from Vietnam. I'm Maks's housekeeping manager. Please, come in.'

Zoe was charmed by him and his soft Scottish burr. 'Nice to meet you, Hamish.'

She walked into a sleek marbled hallway, decorated in tones of dark grey and silver. Understated. Elegant.

She heard Hamish say, 'I'll park the car, boss. Angie said dinner will be ready in about twenty minutes.'

'Thanks, Hamish.'

Maks came and took Zoe's hand again. She must have looked dumbstruck. He led her down the hall and into a sumptuous but again understated reception room. He let her hand go and walked over to an exquisite walnut drinks cabinet. It looked like a piece of art, not furniture.

'Would you like a drink?'

Suddenly Zoe relished the prospect of some fortification. 'A glass of white wine, if you have it?'

Maks came back with a glass of perfectly chilled white wine. He had a tumbler of what looked like whisky. He lifted his glass. 'Cheers. Welcome to my home.'

'Cheers.' Zoe took a sip of wine, appreciating the dry crisp taste.

'Please—sit, make yourself comfortable.'

Zoe looked around. There was an assortment of low couches and footstools set around glass tables covered in the latest coffee table hardbacks. Except these actually looked as if they'd been thumbed through, their edges slightly frayed.

She chose a seat on its own and watched as Maks sat down on a couch at a right angle to her, resting one arm along the back. Utterly relaxed. Yet full of taut crackling energy.

'You have a beautiful home,' she said.

Maks looked around. 'It's probably not what you were expecting.'

Damn his perceptiveness. 'I'm that easy to read?' she asked.

'It's refreshing. I'm used to people freezing their emotions with enough chemicals to put an animal to sleep for a year.'

Zoe couldn't stop a huff of laughter. 'I have to admit I would have expected something less…discreet. Maybe a penthouse apartment.'

Maks made a face. 'That's more my brother Sharif's style. He likes to be far above mere mortals, high in the sky.'

Zoe took a sip of wine. 'What's he like?'

'Driven.'

'What about your other brother... Nikos?'

'He used to live like a nomad, keeping apartments in our various hotels. But all that looks to change now that he's married and settling down. A wife and baby don't really go with a nomadic lifestyle.'

Zoe's insides tightened. Marriage. A baby. *Family.* Her worst fear. Her most secret dream. She shut it down. She'd vowed never to put herself at risk of feeling that loss and pain again, no matter what moments of yearning she felt.

Maks swirled his drink. 'What about you? What kind of home would you aspire to live in?'

Zoe felt like pointing out tartly that she was perfectly happy where she was, but she knew no one could claim that. It was damp, dingy, and surrounded by concrete jungle.

But before she could say anything she was assailed by the memory of a house in Ireland... Dublin. On the coast...high above the Irish Sea. With acres of green lawn. A big golden house with windows like shining, benevolent eyes. Flowers blooming along borders. A shaggy dog.

Her mother, standing on the steps, calling, 'Come on, you two. It's time to go...'

And then her father, lifting her up so high she could hardly breathe, swinging her around and then down, into his arms...

She'd felt so safe. So loved. So happy.

'Zoe? Are you okay?'

She blinked and saw Maks sitting forward, frowning. 'You've gone as white as a ghost.'

Zoe swallowed down the memory. It usually only came in dreams that turned into nightmares. 'I'm fine. I just...'

What had they been talking about?

She forced a smile. 'I don't know where I'd like to live... I hadn't really thought about it. I'm happy where I am.'

Maks was relieved to see some colour come back into Zoe's cheeks. For a moment he'd been afraid she was about faint. She'd looked stricken.

A light knock came to the door. It was Hamish. 'Dinner is served when you're ready.'

Maks watched Zoe stand up, graceful. She walked out ahead of him, following Hamish, and he noted the unconsciously sensual way she moved. A cynical part of his brain kicked into gear. Was it really unconscious? Or was he so jaded that an act of wide-eyed innocence had him hooked like a gasping fish on a line?

Even if it was an act, he told himself, it didn't negate the fact that he wanted her more with each passing moment. And he was confident that as soon as he'd had her she'd lose her allure and her air of mystery. He didn't want to explore her mysteries. He just wanted to explore *her*.

CHAPTER FOUR

ZOE LEANED BACK and wiped her mouth with her napkin. She hadn't eaten such a delicious meal in a long time. Maks's personal chef, Angie, had served up a simple roast chicken and in-season vegetables, followed by the lightest, zingiest lemon tart Zoe had ever tasted.

Angie came back in to clear the plate and Zoe looked at her. 'Seriously, that was sublime. I wish I could cook like that.'

Angie smiled and looked at Maks. 'I like her—she doesn't behave as if the staff are invisible.'

Maks sent a glower at Angie, who left the room smiling, totally unperturbed. Witnessing Maks's easy and egalitarian interaction with his staff made Zoe feel off-centre. Once again, it wasn't the way she would have expected someone like him to behave.

Maks stood up. 'Come into the lounge for some coffee?'

Zoe stood up. 'Sure.'

Dinner had passed easily. Too easily. They'd conversed about topics as diverse as Irish history, politics, and the latest Marvel movie. It turned out they were both Marvel movie buffs.

But there was still an uneasiness she couldn't shake. She'd trusted a man before—someone she'd known since she was young. And he'd betrayed her heinously and almost violently.

She knew even less about Maks, and yet her instincts were telling her she could trust him. That he wouldn't harm her. Physically. Dean had hurt her physically— or had tried to. But he hadn't left any deep emotional wounds. Zoe sensed that Maks posed a wholly different threat.

'What are you thinking about?'

Zoe turned around from where she'd been looking at the books on Maks's shelves, with her coffee cup in her hand. He was sitting on the couch again, sipping from his own steaming cup, looking so gorgeous that he took her breath away.

She came over and sat down on a couch opposite, with a small table in between them. She noted how a gleam came into those silver eyes, as if he knew exactly how skittish he made her feel. How achy…how needy. But also how scared.

Maks kept his eyes on her and put down his cup. He stood up and came around the low table, sat down on the couch near her.

Zoe's insides somersaulted. She desperately searched for something to say.

'What Angie said…about people thinking the staff are invisible…who was she talking about?'

Great—now he'd think she was fishing for information on his girlfriends.

Maks said, 'I host dinner parties here sometimes.'

'I guess I know what she means…most people are dismissive of those in the service industry.'

Maks winced. 'Or they get them fired.'

'That too.'

Zoe couldn't think straight. Couldn't seem to remember what she'd been worried about. Maks was close enough to touch. To smell. To want. Every part of her clamoured to be closer.

Damn him. Why wasn't he taking the lead?

Maks shook his head, a small smile playing around his mouth. 'Your move, Zoe. If you want me, all you have to do is show me. It's not complicated. I can hear you overthinking this from here.'

Zoe wanted to scowl. But even before she knew she'd made the decision she'd put her coffee cup down on the low table and scooted closer on the couch. She couldn't *not*. The clamour in her body had become a sizzle.

She was fixated on his mouth. She reached out and touched it experimentally with her finger, tracing the shape…

Maks was burning up. He wanted to grab Zoe's hand and tug her all the way into him until he could feel every curve of her body pressed against him. Until he was drowning in her sweetness.

But he held back. Something told him that her reticence wasn't an act.

For a moment he had a jolting moment of wondering if she might be—

But that dissolved in a rush of heat when she leaned all the way forward and pressed her mouth to his.

* * *

Maks's mouth was firm under Zoe's. Her breasts were pressed against his chest. It felt like a steel wall. A *warm* steel wall.

His mouth wasn't moving.

Zoe was in too deep now to pull back. Her brain cells were melting. She pressed closer, angled her head slightly. She opened her mouth and let the tip of her tongue explore the closed seam of Maks's mouth.

And that was when she realised the level of Maks's restraint, as he put his hands on her arms to haul her up and even closer, so she was sprawled across his chest, letting him take her weight.

She lifted her head, looked down, aware of her hair falling around her face. For once she wanted to push it back, so she could see him. He did it for her, tucking it behind her ears. It was a surprisingly tender gesture amidst the inferno building in her blood.

It had never felt like this with—

Maks caught her head and pulled it down, so their mouths touched again. Except this time there was no doubt who was the instigator. Even though he was under her, Maks controlled and dominated the kiss with an expertise that made Zoe's heart race.

He opened his legs so she was between them, her lower belly pressed against the place where the evidence of his arousal was hard. As hard as the rest of him.

Except his mouth was soft now, coaxing her to be bolder, more daring. To use him. She funnelled her hands through his hair, holding his head, exploring his mouth as if she'd never kissed a man before. And she hadn't…not like this. Not as if she was an adventurer in a new undiscovered land.

Zoe was killing Maks with a thousand tiny innocent kisses. With the most chaste foreplay he'd ever indulged in. Either she was a wanton seductress who knew exactly what she was doing and was laughing at him for his restrained response, or she really was as gauche as her kisses.

Except gauche kisses had never turned him on like this. He had never been so close to climax with his clothes on.

He moved her so that she lay under him on the couch, looking up at him with those huge sea-green eyes, her hair tumbled around her head, cheeks flushed, mouth plump and moist.

He gritted his jaw when his erection pressed uncomfortably against his trousers. His thigh was between her legs and he moved it subtly against her, seeing how her eyes widened at the friction.

He lowered his mouth to hers again, to find it open, willing. She put her arms around his neck. His chest expanded. He explored the seam of her top above her trousers, delving underneath to find bare silky skin, pushing it up until he encountered the lace-covered swell of her breast. Small, but perfect. Plump.

He squeezed her flesh gently and she gasped into his mouth. A little hitch of breath that ramped up his arousal to excruciating levels.

He tugged on her lower lip, biting gently as he pulled down the lace cup of her bra, his knuckles brushing against the soft swell of her breast. He pulled back and looked down. Her breast was perfect. Her nipple small and hard…pink. He couldn't resist, bending his head and exploring that hard tip with his tongue, feeding her to himself as if she was a succulent morsel…

Zoe was drowning in heat. Sensations were piling on top of sensations so fast she couldn't breathe. Maks's mouth was on her breast, tugging, licking, and it was the most exquisite form of torture she'd ever been subjected to.

Then he was pulling up her top and exposing both breasts to his hands, his mouth.

Zoe's head rolled back. His thigh was between her legs, where she ached. As if he knew exactly what she wanted he moved subtly, so that the sensation spiked like a sharp knife-point.

It was too much… She couldn't get her head around how fast things were moving. In spite of all her rationale, telling herself this was different—way different from what had happened before—she suddenly felt trapped. Very aware of Maks's weight on top of her, holding her down.

She put her hands against his chest and pushed, but he didn't move. Panic flared, eclipsing pleasure. She pushed harder.

Maks pulled back, his eyes molten, cheeks flushed. *'Che cosa, cara?'*

He wasn't even talking English.

Panic was making Zoe fight for breath. 'I can't… I can't breathe.'

Maks reared back. 'Zoe? What is it?'

She scrambled up and back, drawing her knees up

to her chest. She shook her head. Already the waves of panic were receding, leaving her feeling cold and ridiculous. This wasn't the same situation.

'I… I'm sorry. It was just all going so fast… I felt trapped.'

In contrast to hers, Maks's clothes looked a bit rumpled but were still on. She felt dishevelled. Awkwardly, she straightened her clothes.

Maks got up and went over to the drinks cabinet. He came back holding two glasses.

He handed her one. It held dark golden liquid. 'Here, take this.'

She took a sip, watching as he threw the liquid in his own glass back. She winced inwardly. The drink had a warming, numbing effect.

He sat down, giving her plenty of space. 'What was that, Zoe?' Maks looked pale. 'Did you think I was going to…to force you?'

She shook her head, an immediate and visceral rejection of that rising up inside her. '*No*. No. Not at all.'

She couldn't think straight when he was looking at her like that. She put down her glass and got up from the couch, pacing away from Maks. Walking to a window that reflected back her own image. It was dark outside.

She owed him an explanation. At no point had she really felt unsafe or pressured. It had been her own demons.

She turned around. 'Someone else did, though. My ex-boyfriend. I trusted him and he…'

Maks surged to his feet. 'He raped you?'

Zoe looked at Maks. His face was stark. She shook

her head. 'No, but he almost did. I managed to stop him, get him out of my apartment.'

The memory of that awful night made Zoe shiver. The awful full, ugly truth of why Dean had sought her out again.

'Who was he?'

Maks's voice was like steel. In that moment she had a premonition of what it would be like to face a far less benign Maks. She'd faced him once before, when they'd first met.

'Someone from my past. It doesn't matter. He's gone now. He's not in this country.'

Maks was finding it hard to absorb everything Zoe was telling him. She looked so vulnerable, standing on her own, arms folded tight across her chest. The thought of someone forcing themselves on her made him feel sick. But also livid. She was so petite. Slight... He wanted to go over to her, but he felt she wouldn't want that. Not yet.

She lifted her chin. 'The truth is that...as you may have already guessed... I'm not that experienced. In fact not experienced. At all.'

Maks frowned. 'Are you saying that—?'

'I'm a virgin, yes.'

Her words were quick. Clipped. His instinct had been right. A swell of something that felt like possessiveness rose up inside him. Primal. *Mine.* And relief to know she hadn't been subjected to a terrible assault.

She said, 'So, I know that that'll probably change things.'

Maks focused on Zoe. 'Change...how?'

She suddenly looked unsure. 'Well, you won't…you can't find that attractive.'

Maks's body begged to differ. 'Really? And why would that be?'

'Because you're experienced…and I'm not. Most men don't find inexperienced women a turn-on.'

'I'm not most men.' Now Maks folded his arms, bristling at the thought that she was comparing him to her ex. Her bullying abusive ex. He could see her throat work as she swallowed.

'So…what are you saying?' she asked.

Yes, Maks, what are you saying? That you want to be this woman's first lover and risk all the emotional entanglements that come with that?

Maks forced the heat haze out of his brain. He had to be careful. He normally steered well clear of situations like this. He had to let Zoe know the kind of person he was.

'I'm saying that you being a virgin is not a turn-off.'

Quite the opposite, in fact. The thought of being the first man to witness Zoe in the throes of passion was seriously sexy.

'But,' he added carefully, 'I'm not interested in a relationship. I don't do happy-ever-afters, and after my experience with my parents I have no desire to recreate that toxic scenario in marriage. You need to know that.'

Zoe looked at him for a long moment. There was no discernible expression on her face, which unnerved him. He'd believed her to be as easy to read as a book.

She seemed to hug her arms around herself even tighter and she said, 'That's the last thing I'm looking for. Believe me.'

He did. There was something stripped away in her voice, leaving it bare and compelling.

Then she said, 'I think I'd like to go home now.'

Maks was surprised at the strength of the feeling of rejection that rose up inside him at the thought of her leaving, but he forced himself to say, 'Sure. I'd take you home, but I'm over the limit. I'll have Hamish drop you back.'

The fact that Maks was willing to let her leave so easily made Zoe feel all at once relieved and disappointed. She'd just humiliated herself spectacularly by revealing she'd been abused in a relationship, and then told Maks how inexperienced she was. And, damn him, he hadn't reacted the way she might have expected.

She was learning that this man didn't do anything she expected.

But the fact that he was so willing to let her go told her that he was done. As he'd said, he didn't do relationships. And he obviously suspected that, as a virgin, she'd want more from her first lover. Even though she'd denied it.

Zoe just wanted to leave now, and take her humiliation with her. She was about to protest that she didn't need a lift but, as if connected with his boss telepathically, Hamish appeared and started to put on a light puffer jacket.

'It's no problem to give you a lift home, Zoe.'

She couldn't help feeling that Hamish had done this before—sprung into action to help Maks dispose of a woman he was no longer interested in. She followed Hamish and turned at the front door to face Maks. She felt awkward. Why had she blurted all that out? She could have made something up.

She forced a smile in Maks's general direction. 'Thank you for this evening. I had a nice time. It was lovely to meet your sister—she's nice.'

'She liked you too. Goodnight, Zoe.'

Zoe had to restrain an impulse to study his face and imprint it on her brain for ever. And somehow she knew she didn't need to do that. He would be hard to forget.

After Hamish had dropped her at her flat, Zoe sat on her bed feeling deflated. Hollow. She opened up her laptop and did what she'd been reluctant to do before, because that would have meant she was interested.

She searched online for Maks Marchetti.

As she might have expected, compared to his two brothers, not much came up for Maks at all. There was a handful of pictures of him with women, all stunningly beautiful and accomplished. Which made his interest in Zoe even more unlikely.

There were no salacious kiss-and-tell stories—unlike a recent one involving his older brother Sharif. Nor were there screaming headlines as there were about his other brother settling down, speculating about how long it would last.

Zoe saw some pictures of Nikos with his new wife. She was a tall redhead, and Zoe realised that she looked familiar. She was the woman Maks had been talking to at the fashion event where she'd met him again.

She shuddered to think of being in the public eye like that and felt sympathy for Nikos's wife, who didn't look completely comfortable in the photos.

There were some older pictures of his parents—his

father was tall and dark, very masculine. His mother was tall, almost taller than his father, and very, very beautiful. Blonde with grey eyes. Maks's grey eyes.

Zoe winced when she saw the hundreds of images of Maks and Sasha when they were younger. Coming out of a palatial villa in Rome. Going to school with security guards. Skiing. On beaches. Nowhere had been safe from the paparazzi, it would seem.

One picture caught Zoe's eye. Maks was in swimming trunks, on a beach. He looked about sixteen, tall and rangy, his body only hinting at the adult power and strength to come. He had his hand out towards whoever was taking the picture, his face twisted in anger.

Zoe saw there was a girl behind him, looking fearful, embarrassed, in a one-piece swimsuit, all gangly limbs and braces on her teeth. She looked hunted. *Sasha.*

No wonder he hated the paparazzi so much.

But, compared to his brothers and his parents, Maks had since become a veritable recluse. Evidently he and his sister did all they could to avoid the limelight now, and who could blame them if they'd been hounded like that?

Zoe pushed the laptop away and lay back on her bed. She'd effectively turned Maks off tonight, even if he had been enough of a gentleman to say otherwise.

She told herself she was relieved. Maks was a force of nature. A man who would demand nothing less than everything she had to give. Yet she couldn't ignore the ache at the thought of never seeing him again.

Zoe realised now that she'd never been entirely honest with herself where her ex-boyfriend was concerned.

She'd convinced herself that she'd desired him, but it hadn't been desire. Because now she knew how that felt.

It had been loneliness. Pure and simple. A weak need for intimacy. Weak, because she'd always vowed not to let anyone close enough to become important to her.

She'd only let Dean close because she'd known subconsciously that he couldn't affect her. But Maks did affect her. So it was a good thing that it was over before it had started.

A wave of heat went through her body just from thinking about how it had felt to be in his arms. His mouth on her flesh. And it hadn't just been the physical response he'd unleashed—it had been the other, more tender responses. Emotional responses. The instinctive need to open up. Trust him.

Zoe got under the covers of her bed and pulled a pillow over her head. As if that could help her ignore the sense of loss. She told herself over and over again that it was a good thing Maks wasn't interested in pursuing this—her—further, until she finally fell asleep.

When she woke, bleary-eyed, the next morning, to the persistent silent buzzing of her phone she had to shake her head to make sure she wasn't still dreaming. Numerous missed calls from Maks and three texts.

I'm outside, let me in.

Zoe? Are you there?

Zoe, if you don't let me in in the next ten minutes I'm calling the police.

Zoe scrambled to call him back. 'I'm here… I'm here.'

'I have coffee and cakes.'

'What are you doing here? I thought…' She trailed off.

'Can we discuss this over coffee? And by the way it's raining. I'm getting wet out here.'

Zoe looked out of the window. The rain was lashing. She put down the phone and got up, and pressed the buzzer to release the door downstairs. She heard it open and close. Footsteps. And then Maks appeared outside her door. Huge. Broad. And very wet. Drops of water clung to his hair and his short jacket. He was holding cups of takeaway coffee and a bag of what looked like pastries.

His scent hit her nostrils. Musky and masculine. Expensive. She really wasn't dreaming. He was here. Twelve hours after she'd thought he'd said good riddance.

'Can I come in?'

The smell of fresh coffee hit Zoe's nostrils then and she almost groaned. How did he know she couldn't function before her first coffee in the morning?

She stood back and he walked in and she saw the extent of how wet he was.

'I'll get you a towel.'

She went to her tiny airing cupboard and took out a towel, bringing it back and handing it to Maks, who had put the coffee and cakes on her table.

'Thanks.'

He shrugged off his jacket and draped it over a chair. Zoe took in the fact that he was wearing worn jeans and a light long-sleeved top. Muscles moved as he rubbed his head briskly.

She became very aware of her loose pyjama bottoms and singlet top, putting her arms around her chest. 'I'll just…get changed.'

'Here, take this with you.' Maks handed her one of the coffees.

Zoe grabbed it and ran, still in shock that he was here. When she was in her bedroom—mere feet away, but thankfully behind a door—she breathed out and took a sip of coffee, hoping that might restore a sense of reality.

It didn't. She had the quickest shower on record, dried her hair and dressed in a pair of jeans and a loose, oversized shirt.

When she went back out to the living area Maks had the photo of her family in his hand. They were all pulling funny faces. Her insides clenched. Hard.

He looked around. 'This was you and your family?'

She nodded, longing to take the picture from him.

He put it back on the shelf. 'What happened after the crash? Who brought you up?'

Zoe kept her voice neutral. 'I went into foster care. Both my parents were only children with deceased parents. There was a great-aunt on my father's side, but she didn't want to take me in.'

'That must have been rough.'

Zoe shrugged and avoided Maks's eye. 'I don't remember much about that time, to be honest. I was lucky. I only had two foster homes and they were kind families. I know some kids who went through many more and had bad experiences.'

Like Dean, her ex. Zoe clamped down on thinking about him. It only invited comparisons to Maks and the knowledge that Maks was so much more dangerous for all sorts of different reasons.

She looked at him. 'What are you doing here? I thought last night... I thought I wouldn't see you again.'

He frowned. 'Why?'

Zoe's face grew hot. 'Because I'm not experienced.'

'I told you that didn't matter to me. I thought you needed space. I didn't want to crowd you after you told me what happened to you.' He walked closer. 'Make no mistake, Zoe. I want you. That hasn't changed. And I've told you that I'm not interested in anything permanent. But if you don't want to explore this chemistry between us, tell me now and I'll walk away. I don't beg and I don't play games.'

I'm not interested in anything permanent.

That should reassure Zoe, because of the lessons she'd learnt at the hands of personal tragedy and also her ex-boyfriend.

Her head told her to say she wasn't interested. But first, that would be a lie. And second... The fact that Maks had turned up here this morning, that he *still wanted her,* in spite of her lack of experience... She couldn't fight her overriding impulse to stay in his orbit for a little longer. In spite of knowing better.

She took a breath, felt her heart pounding wildly. 'I don't want you to walk away.' *Yet.*

Maks had to hide the rush of triumph. He closed the distance between them, but stopped just short of touch-ing Zoe. 'I have to go to St Petersburg today for a few days,' he said. 'For meetings and to oversee a fashion shoot. Come with me.'

Maks saw the shock on Zoe's face.

'St Petersburg? That's in Russia.'

He bit back a smile. 'That's geographically correct.'

She made a face. 'But I can't just…leave.'

'You have a passport, don't you?'

'Yes, but—'

'What commitments do you have this week?'

She folded her arms and looked at him. 'One is to find a new job.'

The novelty of a woman who wasn't rushing to acquiesce sent a thrill of anticipation through him. 'All the more reason to come away with me for a few days. I owe you for getting you fired.'

Zoe suddenly looked less spiky. 'I do actually have other commitments. I mind a neighbour's child a couple of days a week, and I do some work for a contracting firm, cleaning offices.'

Maks shook his head. 'I can arrange for your neighbour to have substitute childcare. And as for the office-cleaning job… I refuse to believe that's what you need to do to survive, Zoe. You are young, beautiful and talented. You can have the world at your feet if you want.'

Zoe's chest tightened at Maks's words. She knew very well why she preferred to operate on the fringes, and she felt the sting of shame that she didn't have the courage to take up more space. How was it that this man she barely knew, who was from a world elevated well above hers, could see something in her that she didn't even dare to articulate to herself? It was unnerving.

She admitted sheepishly, 'I don't have any cleaning shifts lined up this week.' She saw a glint of what looked like triumph in Maks's eye and said quickly, 'But I won't go anywhere until I know that Sally's childcare is sorted. I can't let her down.'

'More champagne, Miss Collins?'

Zoe looked up. She'd been staring out of the window at a carpet of fluffy white clouds under a blue sky. She shook her head at the steward. 'No, thanks, I'm okay.'

But she wasn't okay. She was still reeling from the speed with which Maks had managed to secure childcare for her neighbour—childcare that she was happy with—and had then spirited Zoe and her one small suitcase out of her shabby top-floor flat, across London to a private airfield and this sleek silver jet, which was now flying somewhere high above Poland, according to the pilot.

Maks was in a seat across the aisle, long legs spread in front of him while he simultaneously spoke on his phone and typed into his laptop. He'd excused himself when they'd got on board, saying, 'I have some calls to catch up on—make yourself comfortable.'

Zoe couldn't imagine ever feeling *comfortable* in Maks's presence. Fizzing with electricity. Alive with anticipation. Reckless. Heady... The champagne wasn't helping her to feel any less reckless. Or heady. And definitely not comfortable.

What exactly had she even agreed to? An affair? Just because she'd said she'd come with him? Would he expect payment in kind in bed?

Her mind shied away from that. Maks was too controlled, too sophisticated. Too proud. As he'd said from the beginning, she intrigued him, and she was sure that sense of intrigue would fade very quickly once he'd spent more time with her. *Once he'd slept with her.*

Zoe shifted in her seat as a pulse between her legs throbbed at the very thought of him—

'What are you thinking about? You look almost… guilty.'

Zoe's head swivelled around to Maks so quickly she almost got whiplash. She hadn't realised he'd stopped talking on the phone and had put away his laptop. She felt guilty now—which was ridiculous.

'I'm not thinking about anything special.'

The pulse between her legs throbbed again, as if to mock her, and she pressed her thighs together. Maks's gaze dropped for a second, before resting on her face again. She scowled. This ability of his to read her mind was seriously irritating.

Wanting to get his attention off her far too obvious thoughts, she said, 'So what are these meetings in St Petersburg?'

Maks sat back. 'The Marchetti Group has an office in Moscow, but we're interested in the untapped potential of Russian designers, a lot of whom originate in St Petersburg. We're interested in developing the city as another growing fashion hub—not just for designers but for brands.'

'Where was your mother from?'

'Originally St Petersburg, but she moved to Moscow with her father after her mother died and he remarried.'

Zoe thought of the pictures she'd seen. 'She is very beautiful.'

Maks's face became impassive. 'Her whole life revolves around her looks. They're as much of a currency to her as money is.'

'Your sister is beautiful too.'

Maks's gaze narrowed on Zoe. 'You noticed that she hides it away?'

Zoe nodded.

Maks's mouth twisted. 'Our mother couldn't handle having a beautiful daughter who might eclipse her, so she did her best to undermine Sasha's confidence. It's probably the worst thing she's done.'

Zoe felt that tug of empathy for his sister again. 'Maybe she'll surprise you and come out of the shadows when she's ready.'

Maks looked at her and his eyes saw far too much. He said, 'Maybe she will.' And they both knew he wasn't talking about his sister.

CHAPTER FIVE

ZOE WALKED THROUGH the series of palatial rooms that made up her suite at the Grand Central St Petersburg Hotel, right in the centre of the city. As soon as they'd arrived at the hotel, to an effusive welcome from the manager, it had become clear that she would have her own suite. She wasn't sure what she'd expected, but she was ashamed to admit that she'd been feeling slightly trepidatious that Maks would have booked them into the same room.

They were in adjoining suites, though. So, while she had her own space, she was very conscious that a mere door separated them.

The drive from the airport to the hotel had taken them past some of the city's stupendously beautiful domed cathedrals and palaces. Zoe itched to explore, and see the city through the lens of her camera, which she'd brought with her. But for now she was enthralled by the vast suite, and if hers was this impressive she could only imagine what Maks's must be like.

She found the bathroom, laid out in cool marble and gold furnishings that should have looked tacky but didn't. And beside the bathroom there was a dressing room. The rails and drawers were empty and her small suitcase looked a bit pathetic. It highlighted how out of her depth she was in this situation. She had no idea how to play the part of a rich man's...companion.

She giggled at that, and her giggle had a tinge of hysteria. *Companion* sounded so Victorian, when the feelings Maks inspired within her were anything *but* Victorian.

The suite's doorbell chimed at that moment, low and melodic. Zoe sobered up again. She made her way back to the main door and opened it. Maks was on the other side, leaning against the doorframe with an insouciance that came from being born into this world. She couldn't control the wild rush of her blood to see him again. She was as pathetic as her little suitcase.

'How do you like your rooms?'

Zoe feigned a nonchalance she was far from feeling. 'Oh, you know... I think they're adequate for my needs.' Who was she kidding? She could fit her entire flat into the suite about ten times.

Maks smiled, not fooled for a second. 'Good. Let me know if you need anything more than...adequate.'

Zoe looked at him suspiciously, expecting to see a smirk around his mouth, but his expression was innocent.

Then he glanced at his watch, and back to her. 'I've been invited to a couple of social events while I'm here. I'd like you to join me.'

Trepidation rushed back. 'What kind of events?'

'No need to look so wary. They're nice things. I've been invited to the gala opening night of the St Petersburg Ballet Company. They're performing *Swan*

Lake tonight. At the Mariinsky Theatre—one of Russia's finest.'

As a child, Zoe had been obsessed with ballet and, the Christmas before they'd died, her parents had taken her to a performance of *The Nutcracker*. She hadn't been to a ballet performance since then, and every instinct screamed at her to say *no,* to curl up somewhere and avoid the painful memories.

But something else inside her—something new—resisted the urge to protect. To avoid. She was a grown woman now. She could handle a ballet performance, surely?

She shrugged. 'Okay…sure.'

Maks slanted her a dry look. 'Your enthusiasm is bowling me over here, Zoe.'

She blushed. 'No… I mean, that would be lovely.'

He didn't know the demons in her past. In her head. But then she thought of something else, something far scarier.

'I don't know if I have anything suitable with me to wear.'

She'd brought her one and only smart black dress, but that felt woefully inadequate for what was presumably to be a black-tie event?

'There are boutiques in the hotel. I'll have a stylist meet you and help you to choose a couple of dresses.'

'A couple?'

'There's another event at the end of the week—a showcasing of new designers.'

'Oh…' Zoe bit her lip. Her finances didn't run to buying the kind of dresses that would be for sale in luxurious hotel boutiques. 'Thanks, but maybe I can take a look around the local shops?'

Maks stared at Zoe. He wondered if she was for real. She looked so awkward...conflicted. He was used to women from his own milieu, who already owned a wardrobe of suitable clothes, or the kind of woman who would have jumped at the chance to obtain some free clothes on his tab. He should have anticipated this. He was too cynical.

'I don't expect you to pay for the clothes. I've invited you here and I'm asking you to these events.'

Her face grew redder. 'But I won't accept that. I'm not a charity case.'

His conscience kicked hard. 'I know you're not. Think of it as a loan. We'll have the dresses cleaned and sent back before we leave.'

'You're sure?'

'Of course—no problem.'

An hour later, still feeling uncomfortable, Zoe was standing in one of the hotel's very sumptuous boutiques with a stylist who was looking her up and down critically.

Imagining all sorts of meringue confections, Zoe said quickly, 'I'm not really a girly girl. I don't want anything too fluffy or flashy. Dark colours would be good. Simple, discreet...'

The stylist, blonde, tall and beautiful, smiled and said in a charming Russian accent, 'Mr Marchetti warned me you'd probably say that.'

Indignation flashed through Zoe. 'Oh, he did, did he? What's the brightest coloured dress you have in here?'

A few hours later Zoe was severely regretting her impetuous behaviour. She looked at herself in the mirror and a svelte, groomed stranger looked back at her. In a bright canary-yellow dress. It had a low neckline, small capped sleeves, and hugged her breasts and torso. It fell from her waist in a swathe of material.

Above her hipbones were two small cut-outs, revealing her pale skin. She'd been about to protest when she'd tried it on in the boutique, but when she'd seen it in the mirror she hadn't been able to get the words out to say no. It reminded her of a fairy tale dress, and she'd stopped thinking of fairy tales a long time ago... But not today.

A couple of women had arrived before she'd been able to leave the boutique and had proceeded to do things to her hair and face. And now...

Zoe's chest hurt. She wasn't a stranger to herself at all. That was the problem. She looked like an old picture she had of her mother. Her hair was down but in sleek waves, heavy over one side. Red lips. Her eyes looked huge and very green.

She was too distracted to think of her scars and wonder if they marred the picture.

There was a knock at her door. Too late to change now, or to make excuses. Or worry about her scars.

Full of emotions she'd successfully kept locked up for years, Zoe turned and picked up the small matching bag and wrap. She hoped Maks wouldn't see how exposed she felt.

But when she opened the door every last thought, concern and emotion was incinerated to dust. Maks Marchetti in a classic black tuxedo was simply…breathtaking. Like…literally. She couldn't breathe. The suit was moulded to his powerful body, as if a tailor had lovingly made it especially for him. Hugging muscles and accentuating the width of his chest.

She was barely aware of his grey eyes sweeping up and down, or the way his jaw clenched. Somehow she remembered to suck in oxygen as she raised her eyes to his face with an effort. 'Hi.'

He was shaking his head, 'You look…stunning, Zoe.'

Zoe was still in too much shock to take that in properly.

When he held out his arm and said, 'Shall we?' she put her arm through his and let him guide her down to the lobby, where people turned and stared at them.

She felt as if she was floating. The dress swirled around her legs as she walked—slightly gingerly in the high-heeled sandals. A car was waiting outside and the driver held open the back door, closing it behind her when she was in. Maks got in on the other side. They were cocooned in soft leather and tinted glass, making the world outside seem very far away.

The streets in St Petersburg were very wide. Summer was tipping into autumn, and Zoe noticed golden tinges on foliage appearing everywhere. She could only imagine how beautiful it would look when autumn descended fully.

She was trying to avoid looking directly at Maks. It was like looking at the sun. His beauty burnt her retinas.

They turned a corner and drove alongside a canal. 'I didn't expect so much water,' Zoe remarked.

'St Petersburg has been likened to Venice, with all its canals and the River Neva. There are over three hundred bridges here.'

She shifted in her seat, feeling acutely self-conscious beside Maks, thinking about all those other women she'd seen him with in photographs. Looking far more comfortable than she felt right now.

'Zoe?'

'Hmm?' She kept looking resolutely out of her window, as if the architecture of the city was keeping her utterly enthralled.

'Zoe, look at me.'

She bit her lip, wishing for a second that she had some glasses that would turn Maks blurry, so she wouldn't have to take in his sheer gorgeousness. She turned around and steeled herself, but nothing could help. The fact that he was close enough to touch... *smell*... Zoe gritted her jaw.

He reached out and pushed back her hair a little. 'You don't have to hide, you know. You're a beautiful woman.'

She thought of how she'd insisted the hair stylist leave her hair down and immediately felt defensive. 'I'm not hiding.'

Maks took his hand away and she felt contrite. She wasn't used to compliments, even though she knew this was probably just part of Maks's repertoire. Nothing special.

'I don't mean to sound short. The truth is that I've

never worn an evening gown before. I've never had occasion to. This is all just…new to me.'

'You didn't have a school prom? Or whatever they have in Ireland?'

Zoe shook her head. 'It's called the Debs—and, no… I left Dublin after my final exams…before the Debs.'

She'd been eager to leave behind sad memories and forge her own life, to follow in her father's footsteps to London and beyond. Put some distance between herself and the ever-present grief. Even though it had been a wrench to leave Dublin, it had felt like the right thing to do.

'You look stunning, Zoe. Really.'

She felt ridiculously shy. 'Thank you. So do you.'

Maks reached for her hand and held it. He brought it towards his mouth and pressed a kiss to her knuckles. Everything in her clenched in reaction.

He looked over her shoulder. 'We're here.'

The car had stopped and she hadn't even noticed. There was a red carpet and lots of beautiful people walking into an impressive nineteenth-century building—one of Russia's foremost classical theatres.

Maks got out and helped her out of the car, keeping hold of her hand as he led her towards the entrance. Photographers lined each side of the red carpet, yelling in Russian. She recognised Maks's name being called.

He ignored them, walking past all the other people posing and preening. Zoe didn't mind. She was only too eager to escape the flashes of light. It was very intimidating.

But not as intimidating as the interior of the building. It was breathtaking. As if they'd stepped back in time. Vast spaces and high ceilings. Elaborate plaster-work and chandeliers. Zoe felt dwarfed—especially beside Maks.

Maks was very aware of Zoe's hand in his. It felt small. Delicate. But strong at the same time. A little voice asked him what he was playing at. He never usually indulged in PDAs, or went to these elaborate lengths to seduce a woman. *A virgin!*

Normally he shied well away from any woman who didn't understand how things worked. His lovers had a good time and moved on. No promises, no demands. No games.

That was how Maks had managed to keep such a low profile in comparison to his brothers. And a low profile suited him fine. He didn't have Nikos's need to scandalise the public—albeit he was doing it less now—or Sharif's desire to make everyone bend to his will. He was happy to take a more laid-back role, cultivating and managing the Marchetti brand and its fashion wing, restoring vital respect after the damage inflicted by their father, who had died in the arms of his latest lover. A sordid detail they'd managed to keep from the press at the time.

So any connection with a woman beyond the purely superficial was anathema to Maks. He had a close relationship with his sister and that was all he needed. She got it—she understood—because she'd also witnessed the bitter chaos of their parents' marriage and divorce. Neither of them wanted a replay of that drama in their lives.

And yet here he was…holding Zoe's hand and feeling protective. *It was her first time in an evening gown.*

Maks had been having doubts earlier, wondering if he'd done the right thing, inviting her to St Petersburg—but then she'd appeared in that dress and he'd forgotten every whisper of doubt.

The fact that she'd chosen yellow had punched him in the gut, because he'd known immediately that she'd done it purely to surprise him and was probably feeling self-conscious.

He looked down at her now. The dress showcased her body—her small waist and gently flaring hips, the modest swells of her breasts. Maks remembered how they'd felt in his hands, under his tongue, and his body surged into hot life. As if he had no control over it.

Her gaze was lifted to the ceiling, rapt. The sleek hair and make-up only enhanced what he'd seen that first day. He found it almost impossible to see her scars now, and not because they were covered. They were too deep to hide, but she eclipsed them.

He squeezed her hand. 'Okay?'

She looked at him, and for a second he saw something unguarded in her eyes, but then she pulled her hand out of his and said brightly, 'Yes, fine. This place is…amazing.'

Maks curled his hand into a fist and put it into his pocket, feeling strangely off-centre. He hadn't expected that. Then he mocked himself. He was concerned that Zoe might expect too much or get hurt, but at every step of the way she demonstrated her independence. She might be innocent, but she wasn't naive.

* * *

Zoe hadn't known that Maks could speak Russian, although it made sense, his having a Russian mother. He was speaking it now, to another man, at the drinks reception before the performance started.

She had to admit that Maks speaking Russian was seriously sexy. As if he wasn't already sexy enough. And she couldn't fault him for excluding her. He'd introduced her in English to his acquaintance, but the other man had apologised profusely and claimed his English was not good.

Zoe didn't mind. She was happy to people-watch and revel in the fact that she wasn't the one serving the drinks on this occasion. She knew it wouldn't last long, so she was enjoying it while she could.

They were soon moved to the main auditorium, and when they went into their private stall Zoe stopped in her tracks. She'd never seen such magnificent opulence in her life. There were at least four tiers of seating around the auditorium, reaching high into the gods. The ceiling was frescoed with angels and cherubs dancing around a spectacular central chandelier.

'Wow…' was all she could manage.

Maks said, 'My mother was here on a shoot once, and for some reason she brought myself and Sasha with her—which was not usual. We were normally left with the nanny. I remember seeing it for the first time and being blown away.'

Zoe looked at Maks. They were in a private booth, just to the left of where the main elaborate box was situated, facing the stage. Maks had told her it was the box reserved for local officials.

'You seem very comfortable here in St Petersburg.'

Maks shrugged. 'In spite of my mother I have an affinity with Russia. I guess it's where my roots are. And I have always loved the Russian writers, whereas Sasha prefers the French classics.'

'It's nice that you're so close.' Zoe felt that pang again, thinking of her lost brother.

Maks's mouth quirked. 'She complains that I'm overprotective, but she's my baby sister.'

'My brother would be twenty-three now. I often think about him and wonder what he'd be like.'

Maks took her hand just as the lights went down. 'I'd wager that he'd be a lot like his sister. Independent, passionate...'

Zoe was glad the lights had gone down, Maks's words had affected her more than she liked. She knew she should pull her hand away from his as an expectant hush settled around them, but she couldn't.

Then the curtain went up and Zoe forgot everything around her—even Maks—as the powerful music and the performance swept her up in a lush and magical embrace.

'You enjoyed it, then?'

Zoe scowled at Maks and saw him smirk. They were in the back of his car, leaving the Mariinsky Theatre behind. She'd been bawling like a baby at the end of the performance, and she knew well that her overload of emotion had come more from the memories it evoked than the actual performance itself—which had been spectacular.

'It was amazing. Thank you. Although I think all the

work the make-up artist did has probably been washed away.'

Maks looked at her. 'You look perfect.' Then, 'Did people comment on your scars when you were growing up?'

Zoe was taken aback by the abrupt question, but she also appreciated it. She hated it when people looked at her scars but said nothing.

Absently she touched the one at her lip, tracing the indentation. She dropped her hand. 'Sometimes, in school, they called me Scarface.'

'Children can be cruel. Were you ever tempted to try and get rid of them?'

Zoe looked at him. 'With plastic surgery?'

He nodded. 'Not that I think you need to—at all. But I could understand the temptation…for an easier life.'

Zoe shook her head. But then her conscience made her admit, 'I thought of it when I was younger. In secondary school. But I knew I couldn't be so weak.'

Maks turned to face her. 'Weak?'

Zoe resisted the urge to touch the scar above her lip again. 'They're a reminder of what happened. Of what I did.'

'What you did?'

'I was looking at the camera in the back of the car— it was my father's prized possession. He was telling me to be careful…he took his eyes off the road for a second…and then…' *Bam*.

Maks shook his head. 'Zoe, you weren't responsible for the accident. You were eight.'

Old wounds ached. 'I distracted him. If I hadn't had his camera…'

'Accidents happen. They're tragic. Senseless. And usually the sum of a lot more than just a father taking his eyes off the road for a second. You can't hold yourself responsible.'

Zoe couldn't escape Maks's grey eyes. On a rational level she knew he was probably right. But on a deep cellular level, where her trauma lay, it was hard to believe what he was saying. The guilt had been such a constant companion in her life.

The car had pulled to a stop not far from the theatre. Zoe looked outside, welcoming the distraction. She could see water glinting under the moonlight. 'Where are we?'

Maks was enigmatic. 'You'll see.'

He got out and came around to help her out of the car. Zoe sucked in a breath of surprise, all painful recent thoughts fading back where they belonged. There was a small boat with a glass roof bobbing on the canal. Candles flickered inside, and Zoe saw a table set for two. A waiter dressed in a suit. Waiting...

'We're going on a boat?'

'A little late-night dinner while we take in the sights.'

Zoe was speechless.

Maks took her hand and led her down some steps, where a man helped her on board. She took off her sandals after wobbling precariously in her heels. The boat was small but enchanting. Maks was pulling out a chair, and bowed towards her like a maître d'. She sat down, and the boat starting moving gently along the canal as staff served them chilled champagne and a selection of Russian food.

Zoe realised she was starving as she tried delicious

kebabs, dumplings filled with meat, puff pastries filled with cheese and then, of course, the ubiquitous caviar on small pieces of crusty bread. It tasted salty and sharp and she washed it down with champagne.

'Do you like it?' Maks asked.

Zoe wrinkled her nose. 'I think it might grow on me.'

She was feeling light-headed from the wine, and then dessert was served—delicious blinis filled with choco-late syrup.

While they were winding their way along the canal Zoe asked about various landmarks and Maks told her what they were. One in particular caught her eye, an elaborately domed and turreted cathedral, floodlit.

'That's the Church of the Saviour on Spilled Blood. It's where Tsar Alexander the Second was assassinated.'

Zoe shivered at that gruesome image.

'We'll go and see it tomorrow. The interior has beautiful mosaics.'

Her heart leapt. She ignored it. 'Don't you have meetings? Please don't feel like you have to babysit me. I don't mind looking around on my own.'

Once again Maks wondered what he was doing—actively upsetting his own hectic schedule—but the truth was that watching Zoe's reaction at the ballet had been more engrossing than anything he'd experienced in a long time. He was used to people hiding their emotions or reactions. He was jaded and the people around him were jaded.

'It's fine,' he said. 'It's a fashion shoot tomorrow. I'm sure they'll survive without me.'

* * *

When Zoe woke the next morning, dawn was breaking outside. She stretched in the massive bed. She was
alone. She wasn't sure what she'd expected last night,
but she'd assumed Maks would expect her to go to bed
with him.

She'd certainly been feeling susceptible after that
surprisingly thoughtful boat trip and dinner. When
they'd got off the boat he'd insisted on carrying her
to the car, because she'd still been barefoot. But when
they'd returned to the hotel he'd delivered her to her
door and said, 'I'll collect you for breakfast.'

Zoe must have looked confused, or something worse,
because he'd snaked a hand around her neck, his thumb
brushing her jaw, and said, 'We're taking this slow, Zoe.
There's no need to rush.'

She'd watched him walk away, totally conflicted and
reeling at his unexpected chivalry, but also wondering
why he wasn't trying to rip her clothes off.

Maybe he'd gone off her? Or maybe he was well
aware of his effect on her and was priming her, so that
when he did seduce her she'd be begging him.

She turned and buried her face in the pillow and tried
to ignore the ache of frustration in her lower belly—a
wholly new sensation.

She flipped over on her back again. With Dean it
had been more about the connection they'd had since
they were teenagers, in the same foster home. He'd been
the first boy to kiss her. When she'd left Ireland she'd
broken up with him, and it hadn't been that much of a
wrench. After all, they hadn't even slept together. He'd

pushed for it a couple of times, but something had always held her back.

She'd been surprised at the level of affection she'd felt when he'd appeared in London, asking to see her. She knew now that she'd confused that emotion and her desire with a loneliness that she hadn't wanted to acknowledge.

And Dean had taken advantage of that to sneak under her skin. Convincing her that there was still something romantic…sexual between them. But, as had happened in the past, when he'd pushed for intimacy something inside her had clammed up. She hadn't wanted it.

He'd backed off the first couple of times, but then… that last night…he'd grown angry. Accused her of teasing him. Grown violent. Revealed his real reason for coming back into her life.

Zoe shut the memory out.

Dean was gone. Thankfully she'd managed to get rid of him before he'd done anything serious to her. But she wouldn't forget his horrible, nasty words and the sense of betrayal that had taken her breath away. *'Frigid, stingy bitch.'*

The phone by Zoe's bed rang and she seized the opportunity for distraction.

Maks. Her pulse skipped a beat.

His voice was deep. Sexy. 'Morning. Are you awake?'

Zoe lay back, a delicious sizzle of anticipation in her gut. 'I am now.'

'Be ready in ten minutes. I'm taking you for breakfast.'

She smiled into the phone. 'Has anyone ever told you you're very bossy?'

'Frequently. Now, move.'

* * *

'These *pyshki* are the best in St Petersburg.'

Zoe looked at the doughnuts. She had thought she was full, after the lavish breakfast served in one of St Petersburg's most ornate and oldest cafés, but now her mouth watered again. If she wasn't careful she'd have to be wheeled back to London.

'Here, try one with the coffee.'

Maks handed her a plate holding about five doughnuts and then a coffee. Zoe dutifully took a bite, and as the flaky sweet texture melted on her tongue she moaned. She took a sip of coffee—the perfect accompaniment to the sweetness.

She looked at Maks, casual in dark jeans, top and jacket. His jaw was stubbled, as if he hadn't been bothered to shave that day. It made him look more dangerous. *Sexy.*

She helped herself to another small doughnut. 'So, where to now?'

She was surprised at how much she enjoyed just spending time with Maks. He was easy company for someone who made her insides knot with need whenever he looked at her.

'I thought we could—' He broke off and picked his ringing mobile phone out of an inside pocket. He answered it. 'Yes?' He frowned. 'Okay, tell Pierre I'll be right there.'

'What's up?' Zoe asked.

Maks made a face. 'I have to go to the fashion shoot. Our very temperamental famous photographer is freaking out because his assistant has got a bug and couldn't come in.'

Zoe was shocked at the level of disappointment she felt. 'Oh, that's okay. You should be working anyway. I can go back and get my camera and look around the sites myself.'

'Come with me. You said you were interested in fashion photography.'

Zoe was shocked. 'I couldn't... I mean...really? Would that be okay?'

Maks shrugged. 'Why not? Probably be good for you to see an egotistical maestro in his natural habitat and use it as a lesson in how not to be.'

On the way over to the shoot, excitement fizzed in Zoe's belly. 'Why do you hire people like this photographer if he's so horrible?'

'I didn't want to hire him—the brand insisted. But I'm not suffering people like him for much longer. There's no need to behave like a petulant child, no matter how talented you might be.'

Zoe agreed.

They arrived at a street that was cordoned off by Security, who let them in. Their driver parked up at the back of a long line of trucks and Winnebagos. There was even location catering. Zoe was totally intimidated by the sheer scale. For *one* fashion shoot!

Maks held her hand and led her to the other end of the street, where it opened out into a small square circled by tall neo-classical buildings in varying pastel hues and elegantly crumbling splendour. Zoe appreciated the aesthetics immediately, and could see why this location had been chosen to shoot the models, who were wearing vibrantly modern monochromatic clothes.

Maks went straight over to where a group was huddled around a tall man with long hair, who looked furious. He saw Maks.

'About time, Marchetti. What are you going to do about this? I have no assistant! I can't be expected to work without help.'

Maks's voice was completely relaxed, but a thread of undeniable steel ran through it and Zoe noticed how people's eyes widened. 'This is an unforeseen event, Pierre. How can we make it right and get on with the shoot?'

'Get me an assistant! Right now!'

Zoe had only the barest premonition before Maks squeezed her hand and said, 'Pierre, I'd like you to meet Zoe Collins—your assistant for the day.'

Zoe's mouth dropped open. She looked at Maks, who was looking at the photographer, daring him to disagree. The other man looked at Zoe and sputtered, 'But…who *is* she? Your latest girlfriend? Does she know one end of a camera from the other? This is out—'

'Yes, she does. She's very talented, actually, and actively looking for experience.' Maks's calm voice cut through the photographer's outraged bluster. 'So what will it be, Pierre? Are we going to delay the shoot further or will you let Zoe assist you? Do I need to remind you we only have this location for one day?'

There was no doubting who was in control now.

Pierre looked around, as if to find support, but everyone just looked fed up and eager to get started. Eventually he huffed and said, 'Fine—but I'm warning you. If she can't keep up, I'm leaving, and you can use her to take the shots. I'm sure the brand would love that.'

Zoe heard Maks say something rude under his

breath. Pierre was looking her up and down. He rattled off a list of things he needed and, knowing that this was an opportunity that wouldn't come along again, Zoe let go of Maks's hand and went over to where the equipment had been laid out.

CHAPTER SIX

PIERRE GARDIN HANDED Zoe a card. 'If you're ever looking for more work or experience, give my office a call.'

Zoe bit back an urge to say, *Thanks, but no thanks,*
and said, 'Okay. And thank you for giving me a chance.'

'You know your stuff. You say you're self-taught?'

Zoe nodded. 'My father was a photographer.'

'Who was he? I might have met him.'

Before Zoe could avoid answering that question she
felt a presence behind her. *Maks.* She'd been aware of
him all day on the sidelines, watching carefully.

'If you're finished with Zoe?'

Pierre looked at Maks, a twinkle in his eye. It was
scary how he'd transformed from raging to benevolent—a temperamental maestro, indeed.

'Sure, she's all yours, Maks.'

Maks took her hand and led her away. Zoe waved
goodbye to the other crew and models, who had all
been very sweet with her. She felt buoyed up, fizzing
with energy.

When they got back to Maks's car and sat in the back
she faced him. 'Thank you so much for giving me that
chance. It was terrifying…but amazing.'

Maks's mouth tipped up. 'I've never seen Pierre conduct a shoot without having at least one tantrum directed at his assistant, but he couldn't seem to find fault with you.'

Zoe made a face. 'That could have had something to do with your presence.'

Maks shook his head. 'You're a natural, Zoe, and more qualified than you think. After today, do you still want to do it?'

She nodded. 'Yes. More than ever. Except…' She trailed off, conscious that Maks might not really be all that interested in what she was saying.

But he prompted her. 'Except what?'

'Except I'm not really interested in promoting the façade of perfection. I'd love to work with models who are unique and diverse. Promote a healthier ideal. Not just size, but skin colour, scars… Handicaps. I really admire the model Kat Winters.'

Maks said, 'She's the supermodel who had the accident and lost her leg?'

Zoe nodded. 'Below the knee, yes. She's inspirational.'

Maks smiled. 'I think the industry could benefit very much from someone like you. Perfection is boring.'

Zoe felt self-conscious. She wanted to divert attention back onto Maks. 'Did you always want to go into the family business? Did you have other ambitions?'

Maks looked at Zoe. He wasn't used to people asking him such direct questions.

As if sensing she'd overstepped, she blushed and said, 'It's okay, it's none of my business—'

But Maks took her hand, stopping her words. She looked at him with those huge eyes, still sparkling with excitement and wonder. Things he rarely saw in anyone any more. The realisation that he felt a level of intimacy with her when they hadn't even slept together should make him uncomfortable. But it didn't.

He said, 'For a long time I wanted nothing to do with the business. I hated my father that much. But I expended so much energy hating him and protecting my sister that I didn't leave much space for figuring out what I wanted. When our father died, my brother Sharif called a meeting with Nikos and me. He made me realise that the business was now ours. And that we had a duty to rebuild the name with respect and honour—things that my father had decimated through greed and debauchery.'

Maks's mouth twisted.

'Even though we didn't grow up together, and I wouldn't call us close, Sharif had done his research, and put us in positions that played to our strengths. Nikos took over the PR and hospitality side, and he gave me the fashion and brand side to work with. I think the fact that he wanted to work with us...trusted us... had more of an effect than either Nikos or I expected. Sharif could have taken over the company alone, but he didn't. And I do enjoy what I do... I enjoy the challenge of dragging this company into the twenty-first century. It's about so much more now than just image. Things are changing, and people like you will be at the forefront of that change.'

Zoe's eyes were wide. Maks felt a prickle of exposure. He'd never told anyone all that before. He'd never really articulated out loud what it had meant for his brother to show such trust in him.

He realised the car had stopped outside the hotel. He hadn't even noticed.

Maks's phone rang.

Zoe blinked.

Maks answered the call as he got out of the car and came around to help Zoe out. Her hand slid into his and fitted there in a way that had him wanting to drag her to a private space so he could shut out the world entirely and expose her need for him. He wanted to feel her under him, all around him, milking his body until he didn't have to acknowledge that she did something to him that no other woman ever had.

But it would have to wait.

He made a face. 'That was Sharif on the phone. I have to call him back and make a few other calls. I might be a while.'

Zoe battled a sense of disappointment that was mixed with relief. She hadn't expected that conversation just now to reveal so much of herself, or to hear him reveal what he had. It made her feel as if a layer of skin had been pulled back.

She said, as brightly as she could, 'Don't worry about me. I'll probably have an early night—the adrenalin is catching up with me.'

When Zoe got back to her room she leant against the door, taking a breath. Maks was so…distracting. All-consuming. He demanded nothing less than total investment. Even during the day today, when she'd been concentrating so hard on keeping Pierre happy, she'd been aware of him. And now she was actually exhausted. And yet at the same time still fizzing with energy.

She ordered a light supper, hoping that might help dissipate the energy, but when she'd finished she felt the same. Tired but alive.

She'd worked on her first photo shoot today!

A sudden idea popped into her head and she changed into her running clothes. She realised it was too dark to head out onto the streets of an unfamiliar city, so she pulled her hair into a ponytail and went in search of the gym, which was in the basement of the hotel.

At this time of the evening it was empty, and Zoe warmed up before heading towards a punchbag. She hated the gym, but she loved running and she loved boxing.

After a solid ten minutes of throwing high kicks and punches at the bag, Zoe felt her muscles starting to burn and her face was hot. She hadn't heard a sound, so when a voice came from behind her to say, 'Fancy a sparring partner?' she almost jumped out of her skin.

She whirled around, breathing heavily. Maks was standing a few feet away, with a small towel around his neck, in sweatpants and a T-shirt that left little to the imagination.

'Um...' It was hard to speak when she was hyperventilating. 'I need a break and some water...you go ahead.'

On wobbly legs Zoe went over to a nearby water machine and took off her gloves, poured herself some water. She took a big sip before she dared to look around again. Maks was squaring up to the other punchbag, gloves on his hands.

He said over his shoulder, 'I rang your room but there was no answer, I figured you were asleep.'

Zoe made some kind of incoherent breathless mumble in response and drank him in greedily while he wasn't looking. Lord, but he was beautiful. All taut, coiled energy. Graceful, too, for such a big man. His technique was perfect—he was clearly experienced.

When she'd cooled down a little, Zoe put her gloves on again and went back to her punchbag. Maks was still pounding his bag, lost in his own world. Zoe almost felt she was intruding.

She got back to her own workout, but was too aware of Maks in her peripheral vision. He stopped and she heard him breathing. She tried to pretend that every cell in her body *wasn't* swivelling towards him like the bud of a flower opening to the sun.

'You're good.'

She stopped and turned around. She shrugged. 'Not in your league. There's a boxing gym near me. I started to go there after—' She stopped, feeling the creeping shame she always felt when she thought of her weakness.

'After your ex-boyfriend?'

Maks's voice was like steel.

Zoe nodded. 'I went to learn self-defence, but I found sparring and boxing surprisingly satisfying.'

Maks tugged off his gloves and picked up a couple of punch pads. 'Come on—practice on me.'

'I'm not that good...really.'

Maks started to move around her. 'Come on, Collins, show me what you've got.'

Zoe rolled her eyes but took up her stance, trying to

remember to stay on the balls of her feet and mobile. Maks started off easy on her, but as she matched him he got faster and more unpredictable, forcing her to duck and react more quickly.

Finally he stopped and stepped back. They were both breathing heavily. Zoe more than Maks. She wished she could take off her top, but she only had a sports bra underneath.

As if reading her mind, though, Maks put down the pads and pulled off his own shirt. He must have seen the look on her face. 'Do you mind?'

Zoe shook her head as a roaring sound drowned out everything else. It was the blood in her body rushing to every erogenous zone. She'd seen men in states of undress in the gym—it was normal. But never one like this...

Maks was not human. He was too beautiful to be human. His powerful torso was a finely etched work of art, ridged with muscles. Not an ounce of spare flesh. Hard. Unyielding. Mesmerising.

She dragged her gaze up and looked at him suspiciously. 'Are you trying to distract me?'

He looked innocent. 'Me? No. Only as much as you're distracting me.'

Zoe nearly guffawed, but then Maks's gaze narrowed on her and drifted down, taking in her heaving chest under the clinging Lycra of her top, down over her belly, hips, thighs and lower legs to where her three-quarter-length jogging pants ended. Normally she worked out in a bra top and shorts, and even though she was more covered up right now, she felt naked.

Wanting to push back against the easy way Maks

could manipulate her body, Zoe knocked her gloves together. 'Ready for round two, Marchetti?'

This time he put on his own gloves and started dancing around her. 'Sure, bring it on.'

Zoe launched a few jabs, but Maks ducked them. She knew he was going easy on her, and that only spurred her on. She took advantage of a split second's hesitation on Maks's part to throw a quick right-handed upper cut. The last thing Zoe expected was to make actual physical contact with Maks's jaw. But she did. And, not expecting it either, he stumbled back and fell over a stool, sprawling onto his back.

Zoe wasn't even aware of taking off her gloves or moving. She was on her knees at Maks's side, her hands on his face. His eyes were closed. 'Maks? Oh, my God, Maks... I'm so sorry. I didn't mean to actually hit you. Are you okay? Where does it hurt?'

'All over,' he growled.

His eyes opened and suddenly his hands were on her arms. The air between them was so charged Zoe was sure she could smell electricity in the air. All she could see was hard sinew and sculpted muscle.

She focused on his jaw, which looked red. 'Your jaw...let me get some ice, or something...'

Maks shook his head. 'Don't need ice.'

He was urging her down and towards him, until her chest was pressed against his.

'What are you doing?'

Maks moved his hand from her arm up to her shoulder and then to the back of her neck. He lifted his head. 'Kiss me better and we'll call it quits.'

Zoe's heart hammered. She realised she'd been waiting for this moment ever since she'd agreed to come on this trip with Maks. She bent forward and avoided his mouth, pressing a kiss against his jaw.

Maks said, 'I didn't mean there.'

Zoe raised her head. There was something heady about being over Maks like this, even though she was aware of the strength in his body and knew that within a split-second she could be on her back with him over-powering her...

'I'm aware of that.'

He arched a brow. 'Are you, now? I'm not getting any younger, Collins.'

She smiled. She hadn't expected this either. Light-ness. Flirting.

She bent down, her mouth so close to his that she could feel his breath feather against hers. She stayed there for a moment, relishing the sense of power she had...but every cell in her body was screaming for con-tact, so she lowered her head and pressed her mouth to his.

At first it was tentative. He was letting her explore... move at her own pace. But she could feel the tension in his form. As if his muscles were swelling against her.

Then all of a sudden, even though she was still on top, she was being kissed. Maks's hand was in her hair, urging her closer, enticing her to open her mouth, al-lowing him access. It would have been impossible to resist and she breathed him in, tasting him, letting him taste her.

Her blood ran hot and fast. She was very aware of the steel-like muscles under her breasts and instinctively she pressed closer, seeking to assuage the ache building at her core.

Maks drew back and Zoe cracked open her eyes. Everything was blurry. She realised that she was sprawled on top of him and his arousal was pressing against the top of her thighs. She'd been moving against him like a needy little kitten.

Mortified, she tried to slide off him, but he held her fast, hands on her hips.

'Where are you going?'

She didn't want to go anywhere. She wanted to stay right here. 'Nowhere…?'

Maks shifted slightly and grimaced. 'Actually, I think we need to move somewhere more comfortable. When we make love for the first time it's not going to be on the floor of a gym under fluorescent lighting.'

Zoe's heartrate picked up. 'Make love?'

Maks looked at her. 'Sweetheart, we're halfway there already.'

He shifted against her subtly and his erection teased the apex of her legs. Damp heat flooded her core. She almost groaned. He was right. *This was it.*

He moved and stood up in a fluid movement, pulling her up with him. Zoe couldn't take her eyes off him. He let go of her hand briefly, to bend down and put on his T-shirt. Then he took her hand and led her out of the gym and into the elevator.

He turned to her as they ascended. 'Are you ready for this?'

Not, *Do you want this?* Because they both knew it was a foregone conclusion. Was she ready?

On one level she didn't think she'd ever be ready for

Maks. Could she possibly live up to what he expected of her? Nerves assailed her. It would be so easy to say *No, not yet.* She knew he wouldn't push it. But he also wouldn't wait around for ever.

She nodded.

'I need to hear it, Zoe.'

Damn him. She lifted her chin. 'Yes. I want this. I'm ready, Maks.'

It should have felt unsexy to be spelling it out like this, but the way he was looking at her was so…intense.

The elevator doors opened with a soft *ping.* Maks almost didn't notice, he was so fixated on Zoe. His body was tight with a need he couldn't remember experiencing for a long time.

Once inside his suite, he pushed the door closed behind him. He'd let go of Zoe's hand and she turned and walked into the room. His gaze tracked down her body, lingering on every dip and hollow. He wanted to taste her on his tongue. He wanted to taste her when she came apart.

She turned around. Her hair was up, exposing her neck and slim shoulders. She looked vulnerable.

Maks held out a hand. 'Come here.'

She hesitated a moment and Maks held his breath. Then she walked over, took his hand. He turned them so that her back was to the door. He cupped her jaw, traced his thumb over the scar above her lip. Then he bent his head and pressed a kiss to it. And then higher, over her other scar, high on her cheek, where it disappeared into her hairline.

Zoe whispered, 'Why are you doing that?'

Maks drew back. Her scent wound around him, through him. Musky. Sexy. 'Because they made you a warrior. Don't forget that.'

Sudden emotion made Zoe's throat tight. She cursed him again silently for his ability to see right down to her most vulnerable spot. She could still feel the imprint of his mouth on her scars. They tingled. She swallowed the emotion and reached up, wrapping her arms around his neck, bringing her body flush with his.

'Make love to me, Maks.' She couldn't disguise the huskiness of her voice—she only hoped he hadn't noticed.

Maks looked serious all of a sudden. 'If you want to stop at any moment, that's okay, Zoe.'

The emotion was back. 'It's okay. I trust you.' The words came out before she even had time to process their full significance.

Maks bent down slightly and then Zoe was being lifted against his chest as if she weighed no more than a bag of sugar. He took her into the bedroom, bathed in the golden glow of a few small lamps. The bed looked massive.

Maks put her down on her feet. He put his hand to the back of his T-shirt and pulled it up and off, over his head. Zoe felt dizzy from his scent. Citrus, and something much deeper and darker.

'Take off your top.'

Zoe pulled her Lycra top up and off. She suddenly felt self-conscious in her very plain sports bra. Conscious that she was less than well-endowed.

She almost brought her arm up, but Maks said roughly, 'Don't do that. Turn around.'

Zoe turned around and felt him undo the bra at the back. He slipped the straps down her arms and it fell to the floor at her feet. She kicked off her trainers.

Maks stood behind her, the heat from his body making her shiver with awareness. Not cold. His hands were on her shoulders, moving down her arms. On her waist, spanning it easily. Then up, under her breasts. Zoe's breath was choppy, and it stopped completely when his big hands cupped her breasts. Her nipples pebbled against his palms into tight points of need. She bit her lip.

Maks's mouth pressed a kiss to the spot where her shoulder met her neck. One of his hands moved down, over her belly, teasing at the top of her jogging pants before tugging them down, over her hips. Meanwhile his other hand was massaging her breasts.

Her head fell back against his shoulder. She could feel the smattering of hair on his chest abrading the skin of her back. She wanted to turn around and feel it against her breasts. Her skin. Except she couldn't turn around because Maks's hand was exploring under her lace panties, and further, to the place where her legs were tightly clamped together.

He said in her ear, 'Let me feel you, Zoe. Let me feel how much you want this.'

She relaxed, and Maks's hand slipped between her legs, his fingers coming into contact with the seam of flesh that hid the beating centre of every nerve-point in her body. He touched her there, until she was helpless but to relax even more, opening herself up to his wicked fingers.

She gasped when he found the moist evidence of

her desire. She felt him tense against her, even as he stroked her flesh until she wasn't sure how she was still standing.

His movements became more rhythmic and Zoe's body responded, moving against his hand, willing him to explore deeper. He was a master of sorcery, penetrating her flesh again and again while he stroked that sensitive cluster of cells. Then, on a cry that came from some guttural place as his other hand squeezed her breast, Zoe's whole body tightened like a vice, before a rushing pleasure exploded outwards and upwards, washing everything she'd ever known away and replacing it with a pure kind of satisfaction she'd never felt before.

She wasn't aware of collapsing against him. She was only aware that he was laying her down on a soft surface and resting over her on both hands.

'Okay?'

She could barely nod. Her whole body was suffused with pleasure. She could feel her inner muscles still pulsating in the aftermath.

She watched through heavy-lidded eyes as Maks took off the rest of his clothes, revealing a body that was densely packed with muscles. He had a boxer's body. Immensely strong, but graceful.

Her eyes drifted down and widened when she took in the most potent part of him. Long and thick. Hard. She could see moisture beading the head and her mouth watered at the thought of running her tongue along his shaft, tasting that moisture.

Somewhere else, where her brain was functioning,

she wondered who she had become. She had thought there was something wrong with her after—

Maks came down alongside her. 'What are you thinking?'

Zoe's face flamed at her outrageous fantasy. Her hair had come loose. 'Nothing important.'

He put a hand on her belly. 'You're incredibly responsive. You seem surprised… You didn't—?'

She cut him off. 'No, not with him.' She wanted to get *him* out of her head. She turned towards him. 'Kiss me, Maks.'

He pulled her close, and as he did so he reached for her underwear, pulling it down and off completely. Now they were both naked. His mouth covered hers and she fell into the deep, drugging pleasure of it.

Maks's hand went between her legs again and, emboldened, Zoe explored his body. Tracing his pectorals, the small disc-like nipples, the ridges of muscle that led down to a flat lower belly, and further…to the pulsing heat of him. Strong but vulnerable. Silk over steel.

She wrapped her hand around him, moving it experimentally, up and down. She felt the moisture against her palm and pressed her thumb there, spreading it over his head.

He reared back, putting his hand over hers.

Instantly she felt gauche. 'What is it?'

He looked tortured. Stark. 'Later we can play…you can torture me all you want. Right now… I need to be inside you.'

Her inner muscles clenched at his words, as if her body was already ahead of her. She took her hand away and lay back, watching as he reached for protection and rolled the latex along his length, sheathing all that silk and steel. For a second she lamented that barrier, and bit her lip.

He came over her, nudging her thighs apart with his. He was all sinew and hard lines and those silver eyes... 'Zoe, I meant what I said. If you want to stop—'

'I won't.' She reached up, overcome with a dangerous rush of tenderness for his consideration.

Maks notched the head of his erection against her. She could feel how slippery she was, and might have been embarrassed—but it was too late for that.

Zoe held her breath as Maks slowly joined his body with hers. She could see the strain on his face. 'I'm okay. Keep going.'

In one cataclysmic movement Maks thrust deeper, and Zoe sucked in a shocked breath at the sudden sharp pain.

Maks stopped. 'Zoe...?'

She felt impaled, as if she couldn't breathe. The force of Maks's body deep inside hers was so alien and yet... utterly *right*. She moved to try and escape the sharpness and it subsided. She breathed out on a shuddery breath. 'I'm okay...honestly.'

Maks moved again, pulling back before seating himself deep again. He did this over and over, letting Zoe's body get accustomed to his.

At one point he said, 'You're so tight...are you sure I'm not hurting you?'

She shook her head, a feeling of awe and wonder moving through her as she felt flutters of sensation eclipsing the sense of discomfort. Tension was spiralling inside her, adding to a hunger that made her move restlessly under Maks. There was no pain now, only a delicious sensation of building pleasure, deep at her core.

Maks's movements became harder, faster. He reached under her and tipped up her hips, and she gasped when he touched her so deep inside she saw stars. She was overcome with a primal need that only this man could fulfil. She was almost sobbing, begging him for something she knew only he could give her, and that was when he reached between them and touched her, just where his own body was moving powerfully in and out.

That was all it took. A featherlight touch and she flew apart into a million brilliant shards of ecstasy.

It was only when Maks felt Zoe's body climaxing around his that he was able to let go. It had taken superhuman strength not to spill as soon as he'd entered her tight, slick body, but somehow he'd managed it. His whole focus had been on making this good for her.

And now…as his own climax ripped him apart, inside out…he knew that he'd never experienced anything as good as this.

CHAPTER SEVEN

WHEN ZOE WOKE, dawn was just a faint pink trail outside. Maks was sprawled beside her, on his front, legs and arms splayed. Every inch of his magnificent body was no less powerful in repose. His buttocks were two perfectly taut orbs, and Zoe felt hot when she thought of all that power thrusting between her legs.

He was facing away from her, and she was glad of that tiny respite. Even in sleep she was sure she would feel as if he could see right into her…to where she was freaking out as the full enormity of what had happened last night sank in.

She'd slept with Maks Marchetti. She was no longer a virgin.

She'd allowed herself to be intimate with someone. Blindly. Without a moment's hesitation. And not just because she'd wanted him so desperately—although that consideration had wiped everything else out—but also, and far more worryingly, because she'd trusted him.

She went cold inside when she recalled saying that to him. *I trust you.* She hadn't even noticed. Not really. Too intent on the hunger clawing inside her, too intent on achieving satisfaction.

But as that sank in now she went colder than cold. All her precious defences, which had protected her even when Dean had gone too far, had crumbled like a flimsy house of cards in the wake of Maks's expert seduction.

She'd allowed him access to her most deeply secret self. Where she was most vulnerable. Where she'd hidden all her insecurities and fears. And now…she had nowhere to hide.

Maks moved minutely beside her and she held her breath, but he didn't move again. Terrified he would wake before she was ready to deal with him, Zoe moved off the bed silently. She found a robe hanging on the back of the bathroom door and pulled it on. Then she picked up her strewn clothes and stole out of his suite, hurrying back down the empty corridor to her own.

When she'd closed the door, she let out a long, shuddery breath. *What had she done?* She went into the bathroom and caught her reflection and winced. Her hair was a wild tangle. Her face was still flushed. Her eyes were bright and sparkling. Belying her inner turmoil.

She remembered him kissing her scars.

Zoe stripped off the robe and dived under the shower, lamenting getting rid of Maks's scent from her body even as she scrubbed herself. She saw the faint red marks where his stubble had grazed her skin. The faintest bruise on her thigh where he'd gripped her as he'd thrust deep.

He'd marked her as primally as if they were animals. And she thrilled to it even as she might try to deny it. *You want to be his woman.* She rejected that outright. There was no way, after initiating a virgin, that Maks would be hanging around to repeat the experience. She'd been a novelty from the start, that was all. And now it would be over.

When Zoe was out of the shower she dried herself perfunctorily and went into the bedroom, dragging out her meagre little suitcase. She dressed in jeans and a shirt and packed the rest of her things, ignoring the stunning yellow evening dress hanging in the wardrobe. The sooner she got out of this fantasy land, the better, before she—

She stopped herself. *Before she what?* Fell for Maks Marchetti?

At that moment the doorbell chimed. Zoe's heart stopped. It chimed again. She went and opened it, not prepared to see Maks on the other side, dressed in jeans and a dark shirt, tucked in. He was clean-shaven and his hair was damp.

Zoe instantly felt weak at the thought of him in the shower, water sluicing over that taut, powerful body.

'Maks? Did you want something?'

His face was expressionless, but she could see that his jaw was tight. 'You could say that. Why did you leave my bed?'

My bed. She shivered at the way he said that. It was so arrogant and possessive.

'I wasn't aware I had to ask permission.'

'What's going on, Zoe? Not long ago you were—'

'I know exactly what I was…doing.' Her face grew hot. She wished she could be more suave about this.

Maks came into the room before she could stop him. The door closed behind him. He looked over her head and she realised he could probably see into the bedroom, where her case was on the bed.

He walked around her and into the bedroom.

She walked behind him.

He turned to face her. 'Going somewhere?'

'I thought I should get back to London.'

Maks was in uncharted territory. He was used to women using intimacy as a means to foster a deeper intimacy. He'd never had a woman leave his bed and try to leave the country.

His insides curdled as a possibility struck him. He turned around to face her. 'Did I hurt you, Zoe?'

He cursed himself. He'd been so careful to make sure she was with him, but he knew at some point he'd been taken over by sheer lust and the whole experience. He'd believed she was with him all the way. He could remember the strength of her untried body clamping around his so powerfully, sending him into orbit. But maybe—

She was shaking her head. 'No. *No.* You didn't hurt me. At all. It was…amazing.' She looked shy all of a sudden. 'I didn't know it could be like that. I thought something was wrong with me.'

Maks had a strong suspicion about where that notion had originated, and felt an urge to simultaneously beat that other man to a pulp and to protect Zoe.

He moved towards her, snaked a hand around the back of her neck. Needing to touch her. 'There's nothing wrong with you—absolutely nothing. You're a passionate woman. I saw the fire in you the first time I met you.'

She looked at him. 'You did?'

He nodded. How could she not see that? But then, he

knew how people could be made to feel insecure—his sister was a prime example.

She pulled back, dislodging his hand, avoiding his eye. 'I think it's for the best that I leave. You're hardly still interested after last night.'

'I know you're not someone who fishes for compliments, but last night was not like anything I've experienced before.'

She looked at him, her cheeks going red. 'That's just because I was a virgin. A novelty.'

'Oh, was it, now? I happen to think it was much more than that. We have incredible chemistry—last night was proof of that. Or are you saying you don't fancy me any more?'

Zoe would have spluttered if she could have. The very notion… Her every cell was aligned towards Maks right now, as if he was true north and her blood was full of iron filings.

'No, I'm not saying that. But maybe it's better to just…end it now before it gets too…' She trailed off.

'Complicated?' Maks asked, and then he said, 'I won't let that happen. I'm not in the business of allowing things to get complicated.'

He sounded so sure of himself.

'Last night felt pretty intense. I'm not experienced, Maks. You do this all the time, and you move on. I'm afraid I won't be able to and that scares me.' Zoe bit her lip and then continued, 'You called me a warrior last night. I'm not a warrior, Maks. Anything but. I'm terrified of everything. That's why I don't commit to anything.'

Maks took her hand and sat down on the bed, pulling her down onto his thigh. 'Your whole family died in one moment, Zoe, it's no wonder you're scared. But you survived. You're a survivor.'

Zoe bit her lip for fear she'd let something else tumble out. The truth was that Maks didn't know the half of it. How guilty she felt for having survived. How her whole life revolved around that guilt and how it had informed all her decisions. She wondered if she'd ever feel free to move on and live a life of her own.

In one way, she *was* safe from becoming emotionally invested in Maks Marchetti. She'd never allow herself to wish for something like happiness with him because he wasn't offering it. And because she didn't deserve it.

Maks spoke, scattering her thoughts. 'I'm not offering long-term anything, Zoe. I'm a loner, and I've been reliably informed that I'm emotionally unavailable. You're confusing emotion with sex. What we shared was intense, but it was purely physical.'

Zoe felt the hardness of his muscles under her buttocks. He smelled of citrus and something more potent. An exotic mix.

'I can prove it to you if you like?' he said.

His hand was on her back, fingers seeking and finding the gap between her shirt and jeans, exploring, finding naked skin. Already she was melting. Breathless.

'Can you?'

She couldn't even really care that she sounded as if she desperately wanted him to prove it to her.

He nodded. His fingers were on the clasp of her bra now, and it was undone before she could take another breath. He pulled her closer, reaching around to cup one bare breast under its lace cup. She sucked in a breath. Her nipple was trapped between his fingers, stiffening into a sharp point of need.

With his other hand he cupped her jaw, drawing her face to his. 'Let me show you how it can be…trust me, Zoe.'

Trust me.

Like last night, those words should be restoring sanity to her brain like a bucket of cold water, but she couldn't seem to make herself care. Maybe Maks was right and all this was purely physical. It would burn out and they would go their separate ways. Right now, Zoe was all too tempted to just trust in Maks—again.

A weakness. She ignored the voice.

She touched his jaw with her hand, before spearing his short hair with her fingers. 'Okay, then, let's do this.'

What was it about him that seemed to ignite some spark within her, an urge to rebel, throw caution to the wind?

She knew she didn't really want to explore the answer to that as Maks's mouth covered hers and he pushed the suitcase off the bed.

It fell to the floor, spilling its contents. She wasn't going anywhere.

Maks looked at Zoe, sleeping on the bed. Morning had turned into afternoon, and he was in danger of forgetting about the outside world entirely. She was on her back, the sheet pulled up to her waist. Her skin was still slightly flushed. Breasts plump, with those small, tight pink nipples. His body reacted to the memory of how they'd felt on his tongue, how they'd tasted. How he could make them harder by sucking…

Dio. What was happening to him? He never, *never* encouraged a woman to stay beyond one night. If they saw each other again it was strictly while their mutual chemistry lasted and through no encouragement on Maks's part. That was why he'd always chosen discreet, independent women.

But he'd never met one as independent as Zoe.

She would be on her way back to London right now if he hadn't woken up, incensed to find her gone. For the first time he hadn't been secretly relieved that a woman had left his bed. He'd felt…irritated. Exposed.

What was happening here was way off the charts of Maks's usual modus operandi. But then Zoe was different. And this chemistry… He'd never experienced anything like it.

They'd spent the morning in bed, and it had eclipsed the previous night ten times over. Maks had never come as hard. Or as often. And he didn't know if he'd ever get used to seeing the look of wonder on Zoe's face when she climaxed—as if she'd discovered some ancient secret wonder.

She was a novice, reminded an inner voice. *Her awe will fade. The chemistry will fade. She's just a woman.*

As if hearing his thoughts, she stirred on the bed and it had an immediate effect on Maks's body. She opened her eyes, slumberous. He watched as she registered where she was, and who she was with, when her eyes landed on him. They narrowed on his chest and then moved down to where his body was reacting forcibly under her blue/green gaze.

She moved over onto her side and rested her head on her hand. For a second she surprised Maks with how assured she looked. But then she smiled, and it was all at once shy and bold. She pulled the sheet back and he could see the curve of her body, the cluster of curls at the top of her thighs.

'Where are you going?' she asked.

He smiled. 'Nowhere.'

The outside world was overrated.

Zoe put her camera to her eye and focused on the stunning mosaics in the ornate cathedral. She'd ducked in here after spending the last few hours walking the streets, taking pictures of people, unnoticed.

She understood why she liked photography so much—it kept her removed. And she was losing herself in photography right now to distract herself from the enormity of letting Maks persuade her to stay when she would have fled. Back to her safe little life. Changed for ever. But safe again.

Really? asked a small inner voice. *Would you have been able to put Maks Marchetti behind you as if it had never happened?*

No. Zoe wasn't self-delusional enough to tell herself that. She would never forget Maks now. He was imprinted on her mind and on her body in a way that truly terrified her. Which was why she'd wanted to run.

Except it hadn't taken much to persuade her to stay. They'd spent a whole day in bed yesterday, ordering from room service. Maks had disappeared in the evening—presumably to catch up on the work he was meant to be doing. Zoe had been too sated and ex-

hausted to do anything but have a shower and go back
to bed.

Maks had woken her a few hours later, sliding into
her bed, wrapping his hard, naked body around hers.
She'd turned to him instinctively, more than shocked
to find how accustomed she'd already become to having him in her bed.

He hadn't said a word, but he had used his mouth
to communicate an urgency and desperation that she'd
matched. Rising above him and taking him inside her,
moving up and down experimentally at first, and then
with more confidence when she'd seen the look of ab-
solute absorption on his face.

The sensation of being in control had been heady.
Until Maks had said, *'Witch...'* and put his hands on
her hips, holding her so that he could pump powerfully
into her body, showing her that any sense of control had
been brief and illusory. But by then she hadn't cared,
because every point of her being had been fixated on
chasing the ecstasy only he could bring.

She groaned softly at the memory and a nearby tour-
ist looked at her. Mortified, Zoe walked back out into the
late-afternoon sunshine, blinking as her eyes adjusted to
the light. Autumn was arriving and the city was taking
on a golden hue. It was more beautiful than she would
have ever imagined, with the multi-coloured turrets of
the church standing out against the bright blue sky.

'Here you are.'

Zoe would have dropped her camera if not for the
fact that it was around her neck. She whirled around,
her joy at seeing Maks taking her by surprise before
she could stop it.

He'd been gone when she'd woken this morning, but had left a note.

> *I can't keep avoiding meetings—much as I'd pre-fer to. My driver will take you wherever you want to go, except to the airport.*
>
> *You promised to be my date tonight, don't forget…*
>
> *M*

His date. For another event later this evening. She'd avoided thinking about it till now.

'How did you find me?'

Maks held up his phone. 'I called the driver—amazing what modern technology can do these days.'

Zoe made a face. He turned her brain to mush. Especially when he was dressed in a dark grey three-piece suit that made his eyes look even steelier.

He said, 'I've arranged for the designers in the showcase to send over some dresses for you to choose from for this evening.'

Zoe walked with him back to the car. He'd told her about this event—a fashion show to showcase up-and-coming Russian designers, get them noticed on the world stage. Insecurity lanced her.

'But I'm not a model—I'm way too short. The dresses probably won't fit.'

'I've given them your size and height.'

Zoe stopped before they reached the car. 'I wouldn't want to let them down, though…what if I choose a dress and it looks awful on me? That's hardly fair on the designer.'

* * *

Maks turned to Zoe. She looked genuinely concerned. When he could well imagine other women being incensed at the thought of wearing an unknown designer, she didn't want to let them down. He felt a curious sensation in his chest.

'Let me be the judge of whether or not you'll do them justice, hmm? After all, it's my reputation on the line—and the Marchetti Group's.'

She bit her lip and Maks had to fight back a wave of desire. He'd found it hard to concentrate today, wondering where she was. How she was after their indulgent day. And night. She'd been innocent. She must be tender.

That had unleashed another wave of desire.

He took her hand and said, with a rough edge to his voice, 'Stop biting your lip. It's mine to bite.'

Instantly her cheeks went pink. She released the plump flesh, moist from her teeth and tongue. She was a novice with the wiles of a siren. An erotic combination that Maks couldn't resist and had no intention of resisting until he was well and truly sated.

Zoe had never exposed so much flesh before. Acres and acres of pale skin. But the dress… It was like a dress straight out of a fantasy she'd always had but had never acknowledged before.

Never allowed herself to acknowledge.

She'd always believed she wasn't 'girly', deliberately avoiding dresses or anything too flouncy, but after a few days with Maks Marchetti Zoe's inner girly girl was unleashed and there was nothing she could do to stop it.

The dress was an exquisite confection of pink silk and tulle. It had a deep vee to her waist in the front, and two slim straps criss-crossing over her back, holding the dress up. A thick waistband encircled her waist, and a layer of sheer tulle fell to the floor over the silk under-skirt, all in the same dusky pink colour. And when she moved the dress sparkled from the thousands of tiny sequin stars sewn into the fabric by hand.

The designer had brought accessories, and friends to do Zoe's hair and make-up, and she was even further out of her comfort zone now, with her hair pulled back into a rough chignon. For the first time she wasn't as acutely aware of her scars as she normally was. Even though they weighed nothing, they were a part of her and they'd always felt like a burden. Something she had to carry.

There was a delicate silver chain around her neck that hung down into the deep vee of the dress, between her breasts. And that was it. Simple. Understated. Elegant. She hoped.

There was a knock on her door and her heart thumped. She picked up the clutch bag from a nearby table and opened the door.

Maks was wearing a white tuxedo jacket and shirt with a black bow tie. The snowy white made his skin look darker. Zoe's mouth dried. That dark grey gaze swept up and down, resting on her chest before moving up. His eyes were wide, his expression arrested.

Immediately Zoe's fledgling sense of confidence threatened to crumble. 'What is it? It's not appropriate, is it? It shows too much…'

Maks let out a sound halfway between a laugh and a groan. 'You could say that.'

Then he must have seen something on Zoe's face. He put out a hand. 'No, it's fine. You'll probably be more covered up than most people there. It's just…you're more than beautiful, Zoe. You're breathtaking.'

'Oh…' She felt her confidence slowly return, along with shyness. She touched her hair self-consciously. 'They put it up…'

Maks reached out and touched her jaw with a feather-light touch. 'I told you…you don't have to hide.'

This was too huge for Zoe to analyse right at that moment—that a man like Maks Marchetti should be the one who was seeing all the way into her and not turning away in disgust or disdain.

She picked up the short blazer-style jacket to accompany the dress and said, 'I'm ready.'

As the elevator descended to ground level, Maks thought to himself that he was glad one of them was ready, because as soon as she'd opened her door and he'd seen that dress he'd wanted to walk her right back into the room, strip it off her body and bury himself inside her until the rush of blood in his brain cooled down enough for him to think straight again.

A short while later Zoe flinched minutely under the barrage of flashbulbs and shouts directed at her and Maks. Before, at the ballet, he'd ignored them and gone straight into the venue, but here he was stopping for a minute to let them get pictures.

She could feel his tension. He resented it. She thought

of what he'd experienced at the hands of the media when he'd been younger. They'd fed off his and his sister's pain. No wonder he despised them and their invasion of his privacy.

When they were inside the building—an old disused warehouse on the outskirts of the city—Zoe looked up at Maks. His jaw was tight.

'Maks… *Maks.*'

He looked at her. Blankly for a second. As if he'd forgotten she was there. It made a shiver go down Zoe's back.

'You can let go of my hand.'

Something flared back to life in Maks's eyes and immediately he released her hand. 'Sorry.'

She shook her head. 'Why did you stop for the photographers just now?'

Maks looked at her. 'Because, as much as I loathe them, they also help promote our business. Suffice to say they'll never get anything more from me than a few seconds.' His mouth quirked. 'If Nikos was here and not a newly married father he'd probably still be outside, preening for them.'

'What about Sharif?' Zoe was glad to see him relax, even as she didn't welcome how much it meant to her.

'Sharif has a similar attitude to the paps as me. When our father kidnapped him—'

Zoe gasped. '*Kidnapped* him?'

Maks nodded. 'His mother took him back to her Arabian home when she realised our father had only married her for her dowry. Sharif lived there with her for nine years, until our father went after him because he was coming of age. As the mysterious eldest son of

Domenico Marchetti, half-Arab, half-Italian, Sharif was subjected to an intense scrutiny that has never let up.'

Zoe absorbed that. But before she could ask Maks any more, they were approached by a waiter carrying glasses of champagne.

Maks took two and handed her one. *'Na zdorovie.'*

Zoe tried to wrap her tongue around that. *'Nostro-via...?'*

Maks smiled. 'Good enough.'

He clinked his glass on hers and they each took a sip. Zoe felt warm under his gaze, and it was an effort to break eye contact and look around.

It was a huge old warehouse—very industrial chic. Catwalks were set up all through the room, with models walking up and down. People in elegant finery milled around, looking at the models, consulting brochures. Zoe spotted her dress designer in the distance, standing near a catwalk and presumably showcasing her designs. Zoe recognised the whimsical romantic nature of her dresses.

A couple of people approached Maks, and that started a constant stream of people over the next couple of hours. Zoe was happy to hang back, but he always drew her forward, introducing her even though his conversations were invariably in Russian or another European language so she couldn't really participate.

Hanging out with Maks made her feel very conscious of the fact that she hadn't gone to university. *But you could have*, pointed out a small inner voice. Zoe knew it was irrational, and probably very stupid, but she'd always felt that if Ben, her brother, hadn't had a chance to go to university and fulfil his potential, then what right had she?

'Okay?'

Jolted out of her momentary introspection, Zoe looked up at Maks. He was alone, his legion of fans and sycophants having melted away. She nodded, and pasted a bright smile on her face. 'Fine.'

He took her hand. 'Liar. One day you'll tell me what you're thinking of when you disappear like that.'

The fact that he'd noticed made her feel alternately warm inside and fearful. Maks saw everything. And she did have secrets. Secrets that she worked hard at ignoring.

Zoe said brightly, 'I hate to disappoint, but I wasn't thinking of much at all.'

Maks made a sound to indicate how much he believed that, and said, 'Ready to go?'

'Can we?'

Maks smiled. 'I'm an expert at showing my face, talking to the right people and then leaving.' His gaze swept her up and down. He suddenly looked hungry. 'Anyway, I've been fantasising about snapping those far too flimsy straps so that you're naked and on my bed in the shortest time possible.'

Heat curled inside Zoe's lower body, flames licking at her core. Breathlessly she said, 'You'll do no such thing. I promised Oksana I'd take care of her dress.'

Maks arched a brow. 'Oksana?'

'One of the designers you're showcasing and supporting?'

Maks rolled his eyes. 'Fine—I won't damage the dress.'

Zoe felt like giggling. She wasn't used to feeling this…light. Bubbly. Emotion gripped her and she pushed it back down. It had no place here. This was just physical. Not emotional.

Maks tugged her towards the entrance. 'Come on—it's our last night in St Petersburg. I want to take you to my favourite late-night café.'

Zoe let Maks bundle her into the back of his chauffeur-driven car and they were whisked across the sparkling city. Soon they pulled up outside a tall, ornate building. Huge oak doors were opened by a man in a dark suit wearing an earpiece. He nodded at Maks, clearly recognising him.

Inside it was dark and mysterious. Zoe saw alcoves with velvet banquette seats. Candles flickered over faces, half-hidden. Low music played. A sleek blonde woman met them and showed them to one of the booths.

Zoe had never felt more transported in her life. They could have stepped back in time to the playground of the decadent Tsars. And that feeling was only compounded when a selection of food was brought to the table. Small baked puff pastries filled with cheese. Blinis rolled and filled with caviar. And desserts: layered honey cake and balls of dark chocolate. All washed down with sweet sparkling wine.

Zoe was drunk on the wine, the food, but most of all on Maks. He sat beside her, feeding her morsels, not satisfied until she'd tasted a little piece of everything. One arm was stretched out behind her and his fingers grazed the back of her bare neck. Making her skin tight and hot. Making her breasts ache and her nipples tighten with need.

He lifted a tiny piece of toast with caviar. Zoe shook her head, laughing. 'I can't. I'll burst.'

'Fine. I'll have it.'

Maks popped it into his mouth, smiling as he ate. The lightness Zoe had felt earlier still infused her. It was heady. Maks had undone his bow tie and it hung open rakishly, the top button of his shirt was undone too, revealing the bronzed column of his throat.

Zoe saw his gaze drop and rest on her chest. She looked down to see the dress was gaping slightly, show-ing the curve of her bare breast. The blood pulsed be-tween her legs, hot and heavy. She looked back up and saw Maks was reaching for her, cupping her jaw and angling her head to take her mouth in a kiss that sent her hurtling over the edge of all restraint.

She strained towards him, her arms around his neck. His hand slid into the front of her dress and closed around one breast, squeezing her flesh, trapping a nip-ple between his fingers. Zoe gasped into his mouth.

He said roughly, 'I want to taste you, right now.'

She drew back, shocked at how desperate she felt. 'Okay.'

Maks smiled and took his hand off her breast. He somehow communicated to the discreet staff that they were leaving, and when he'd paid the bill he led her out on shaky legs to the car.

The journey back to the hotel was a blur. Zoe didn't feel drunk any more. Everything was crystal-sharp.

As soon as they got into Maks's suite he pulled off his jacket and shirt, reached for his trousers. Zoe kicked off the sandals she was wearing. Maks's hands were now on his briefs, pulling them down, releasing his arousal.

Zoe's mouth watered. Feeling bold, she dropped to her knees in front of Maks, the dress billowing out around her on the ground, a cloud of silk and tulle. But she was oblivious to that.

'Zoe…what are you—?'

Maks groaned as Zoe took his erection in her hand and came close. She darted her tongue out, licking the head. Tasting the salty bead of moisture.

'Zoe, you don't have to—'

But she didn't hear what he said because she was taking him into her mouth, running her tongue around the ridge below the head experimentally. She felt Maks's fingers in her hair and she put her hands on his thighs as she explored the silky heat of his body, marvelling at how powerful she felt when she was the one on her knees.

She could feel the tremor in Maks's hand, and the way his hips were jerking as if he couldn't control himself. She took him deeper, relishing his essence, her hands tightening on his thighs as he jerked into her mouth.

Then he was pulling back, out of her mouth, and she looked up. Maks emitted a curse in Italian, or Russian—she wasn't sure which—and then he was hauling her up, reaching under her dress to pull her underwear down.

He lifted her against the door, saying roughly, 'Put your legs around my waist.'

And then he was thrusting up, right into the heart of her. His big, slick body was embedded in hers so tightly and deeply that she saw stars. Zoe clung to Maks as he effortlessly held her, thrusting deeper and deeper, harder… Until Zoe had nowhere to go except over the edge, crying out as her whole body shattered around Maks's.

She was barely aware of him pulling free and the hot splash of his release against her belly, under the dress.

Maks lifted her into his arms and carried her to the bedroom, stripping off the dress and then taking her by the hand into the shower, where she would have sunk to the floor in a state of sated bliss if he hadn't held her up as he lathered soap all over her body and shampooed her hair.

Afterwards he dried her with a huge soft towel. Then he took a robe from the back of the door and wrapped her in it, leading her to the bed, where she lay down, unable to move a muscle.

A few hours later Zoe woke with a start. She sat up, becoming aware of the voluminous robe, and then she remembered that desperate coupling against the door. The taste of Maks's body on her tongue. *In her mouth.* Her inner muscles squeezed at the memory.

The bed beside her was empty. She went out of the bedroom, passing a chair with the beautiful dress draped over it carefully. Her face felt hot when she realised she couldn't even remember Maks taking it off her.

She walked down the corridor, making no sound on the plush carpet, and found Maks standing at the window, looking out at the sleeping city, its lights twinkling in the distance. He was bare-chested, but had pulled on his trousers.

He turned around when he heard her. She walked

over, feeling shy, and stood beside him. She sensed tension.

He said, 'I apologise for earlier… I'm not usually so…uncivilised.'

Zoe turned to face him, surprised. 'You didn't hurt me.'

Maks's mouth firmed. 'Maybe not, but—'

Zoe reached out, touching his arm. 'I liked it.'

Very much.

She blushed, and was glad of the low lighting that disguised it.

He looked at her, and then reached for her, pulling her into his side. 'You did?'

Zoe ducked her head against him, not wanting him to see how much she had liked it. His skin was warm, his muscles hard. She nodded against him, embarrassed by the depth and strength of her own desires.

He tipped up her chin. He still looked serious. 'You're small. I was afraid I'd taken you so quickly that you hadn't had time to be ready, or even to say no…'

Zoe's heart swelled dangerously. He was so much the opposite of her ex-boyfriend, who had ultimately been prepared to use violence to get what he wanted.

She shook her head. 'Honestly, you didn't hurt me. I was…ready.'

And she was ready again. She could feel her body softening, ripening. Just from being near him.

'You're sure?'

She came around in front of him and reached up. Putting her arms around his neck. Bringing her body flush with his. 'Yes. I'm sure. I'm not delicate, Maks.'

She had a sense, then, of her own innate strength.

An awareness that was new and revelatory. Maks had given her this, and it was more priceless than any jewel.

He looked at her for a long moment and then he brought his hands to her hips. She could feel his body harden against her and she shifted against him. The serious look faded as his eyes blazed with renewed heat. Zoe still couldn't believe that she had such an effect on him.

He said, 'This…between us…isn't over, Zoe. Not by a long shot. We have to leave here tomorrow, but this isn't over…'

Zoe blinked. She hadn't even thought about tomorrow. She'd happily let the cocoon of Maks's world enclose her in a timeless bubble. But now something flickered inside her. *Hope.*

'What are you saying?'

He caught a lock of her hair and wound it around a finger. He said, 'I have to go to Venice, and if you want my plane can take you on to London. But I'd like you to come to Venice with me for a couple of days.'

Zoe felt a yearning rise up inside her. It would be so *easy* just to acquiesce. Even though she knew the sensible and smart thing to do would be to end this now. Go back to her regular life. To reality. Which was far removed from this man and his world, where he clicked his fingers and things manifested themselves as if by magic.

But…would it be so wrong to indulge for just a little longer? It wasn't as if he was lulling her into a false sense of security. She knew he was only offering a finite affair. And she didn't want anything more either.

Liar, whispered that small voice.

She ignored it. She was getting good at that. At ignoring her conscience. At ignoring that yearning feeling. Yearning for something she'd shut out for years. *Love. A family.* No. Those things represented loss and pain. She wasn't going to risk that ever again. This wasn't about that. Not remotely. So she was safe.

'Okay. I'll come with you.'

Maks smiled. 'Good.'

And then he bent his head and covered her mouth with his, and she leapt straight back into the fire that was so effective at burning away the voice of her conscience.

CHAPTER EIGHT

Zoe had seen pictures of Venice her whole life. Who hadn't? But pictures couldn't have remotely prepared her for that first view down the Grand Canal from the water taxi. For once, she didn't even feel the urge to look through the lens of her camera. It was just so… beautiful. Timeless. Iconic. Familiar and yet totally new at the same time. Trying to capture it digitally would inevitably do it a disservice.

The crumbling ancient *palazzos* had romantic balconies, and windows that winked like eyes as they passed by. Zoe couldn't help but wonder about the people who had lived in those places….who lived there now. It was like a fairy tale place.

'You're impressed.'

Zoe heard the smile in Maks's voice and glanced at him, feeling gauche. 'Sorry, you're probably used to a more blasé, sophisticated reaction.'

He reached out and caught her hand, tugging her into him where he stood near the driver at the wheel, behind a pane of glass. 'What I'm used to is not necessarily good. It's a privilege to see Venice again through your reaction.' Maks looked at the buildings over Zoe's head. 'I'd forgotten how amazing it is the first time.'

Zoe was glad he was not looking at her as she blushed at his reference to *the first time*. It had indeed been amazing.

The water taxi veered smoothly towards one of the impressive buildings. It stood on its own, with an area of greenery to the side, a massive balcony on the first floor. The taxi pulled up to a wooden walkway and a man in a uniform rushed towards them, helping first Zoe, then Maks, out of the bobbing boat.

They were led up to the foyer of the hotel and welcomed as if Maks was returning royalty by a fawning manager, who came with them in the rococo-inspired elevator up to the most sumptuous, luxurious suite of rooms Zoe had ever seen.

There were chandeliers, gold-painted frescoes on walls and ceilings, acres of Carrara marble, Murano glass vases and lamps, oriental rugs on parquet floors.

When the manager had left, and she'd managed to pick her jaw up off the floor, she asked, 'Do you own the place or something?'

Maks looked a little sheepish.

Zoe's jaw dropped again. 'You own this hotel…' She couldn't quite compute that information, so she walked over to the open double doors that led out to the balcony. She looked down over the Grand Canal and shook her head at the incongruity of *her* in this unbelievable place.

Maks came and stood beside her. 'What are you thinking?'

She looked at him. He had his hands in his pockets,

nonchalant. 'I'm thinking that it was naive of me not to just assume you owned this hotel. It must be amazing…'

'What must be amazing?'

Zoe shrugged. 'To walk into a place like this and know that it's yours… It's kind of incomprehensible to me, and yet it's all you've ever known?'

Now Maks shrugged and looked away, out to the view. He put his hands on the balcony. 'I've had great privilege. I would never deny that. But if I could swap what my sister and I experienced for a far less privileged existence then I would, in a heartbeat.'

'It was that bad?'

He glanced at Zoe, his face stark. 'It was bad enough.'

Somehow Zoe knew exactly what he meant. It had been just 'bad enough' to blight both their lives for ever. Like hers had been blighted—albeit by very different circumstances.

She said, 'I only had eight years with my parents and my brother, but they were wonderful years.'

So wonderful that she couldn't bear to contemplate experiencing having a family again, only to have it ripped away from her.

Maks turned his back on the view. 'You lived in Dublin?'

Zoe nodded and smiled. 'We had a beautiful house on the coast, just south of Dublin city, overlooking the Irish Sea. I used to love sitting in the conservatory and watching the weather change over the sea, especially on stormy days. I'd watch how it rolled in with such a fury, and yet I felt so safe and protected…as if nothing bad could ever touch me.'

What an illusion that had been.

Maks reached out and cupped her face. His thumb traced the scar above her lip with such a light touch she was afraid she was imagining it.

He said, 'And yet it did.'

Emotion tightened Zoe's chest and throat. Maks must have seen it, because he pulled her into his chest and wrapped his arms around her. But Zoe was too scared to let the emotion bubble up and out, terrified it might never stop. So she swallowed it down and pushed out of Maks's arms, avoiding his eye.

'I think I'll go and freshen up.'

Maks watched Zoe walk back into the suite, pick up her bag and disappear into the bathroom. He rubbed at his chest absently. The raw emotion in her eyes just now had hit him squarely in the solar plexus. Normally, any hint of emotion made him shut down in response, but he hadn't been able to ignore Zoe. And she'd been the one to push *him* away.

He turned back to the view of the canal, barely registering it. Which only made him think of Zoe's comment about his jadedness.

Porca miseria. What the hell was going on with him? It was as if as soon as he'd laid eyes on Zoe something inside him had realigned into a new configuration.

Immediately an inner voice said, *Ridiculous. It's physical desire, pure and simple. Unprecedented. Raw. Insatiable. But just desire. A chemical reaction. Not emotion.*

He heard a sound behind him and turned around. She'd changed into cropped jeans and a fresh shirt. Her scuffed trainers. Hair down. Minimal make-up. She looked young and fresh and achingly beautiful. Without even trying.

She was holding her camera and lifted it up. 'I might go out and take some pictures. You probably have meetings to attend?'

Her dogged independence made Maks chafe, when he usually abhorred a lover trying to monopolise his attention. Something rogue inside him made him say, 'Actually, I'm not under pressure today. I'll come with you.'

Zoe couldn't stop the rush of pleasure, even though a moment ago she'd actually been relishing the thought of some space from Maks. He saw too much, and he made her feel too much, but now she felt as giddy as a kid again.

'Are you sure?'

'Unless you don't want me to come with you?'

Zoe just managed to refrain from rolling her eyes at that suggestion. 'No, I'd like it.'

Several hours later, Zoe was drunk again. But not on anything more than Venice, some pasta followed by gelato, and Maks. He absolutely belonged in this milieu, against the dramatically beautiful backdrop of such an ancient and iconic city.

She'd taken a sneaky snap of him on a bridge, and she'd bet money that he'd been a Venetian prince in another lifetime. Albeit one in faded jeans that were moulded to his powerful thighs and taut behind and a dark polo shirt that did little to disguise the lean musculature of his chest.

And aviator glasses that made him look like he'd just stepped out of *Vogue Italia* for men.

Zoe sighed. Whatever anomalous moment or thing had led to Maks finding her attractive, she was sure it wouldn't last for much longer. He turned to her and held out his hand and Zoe's heart constricted.

She was in so much trouble.

As she took his hand and let him lead her into the labyrinthine streets, she knew that against all her best intentions and instincts she'd done the thing that she feared most in the world. She'd fallen in love with Maks. And she knew now that whatever she'd believed she'd felt for Dean had been nothing in comparison. Less than nothing. It had been driven by loneliness, and the fact that she'd known him from her past.

This had nothing to do with loneliness or weakness. It was wild, untameable and elemental. And she knew that whatever pain she'd felt before, even when she'd lost her entire family, would pale into insignificance compared to what Maks would do to her. And she was afraid it was already too late.

Maks looked at Zoe where she stood in the small *osteria* near one of Venice's many bridges. She sipped at a small aperitif. He noticed men looking at her and instinctively moved closer. He'd never felt possessive before.

Zoe looked up at him. 'What was the house that you grew up in like?'

Maks thought of her evocative description of watching storms rolling in over the sea and felt wistful. 'Not like yours. No view of the sea. It was a grand *palazzo* in Rome. Beautiful, but austere. We weren't allowed to touch things because they were all priceless antiques. Once, Sasha and I were playing and she knocked over a vase. I'm pretty sure it was Ming.'

Zoe put a hand over her mouth, eyes wide, sparkling.

'Our father came out of his study and saw it. He took off his leather belt and asked who was responsible.'

Zoe's hand came down from her mouth. Now she looked horrified.

'Sasha stepped forward. She was nine. I think she thought he wouldn't dare, if he knew it had been her fault. But I knew my father by then. I knew what he was capable of. So I pushed her behind me and told him I had done it.'

'He beat you with the belt?'

Maks pulled down the collar of his polo shirt and Zoe looked at where he was pointing, to a faded scar just over his collarbone. A rough ridge of skin. She reached up and touched it. Her finger was feather-light against his skin, yet it burned.

She frowned. 'I didn't notice it before.' She sounded almost angry with herself that she hadn't.

Maks swallowed. 'My father stopped when I grabbed the belt off him and started to hit him. I was fourteen by then, and almost as tall as him. He didn't do it again.'

Zoe took her hand down and Maks missed her touch.

She asked, 'How did you know he would be capable of hitting a young girl?'

Maks's insides felt like lead. 'Because I'd seen him hit one of our young maids. And I'd seen him hit our mother when I was much younger, before they divorced.'

'I'm sorry you experienced that.'

Maks took her hand back and kissed her fingers, relishing their coolness. 'I think I would have liked your house.'

Zoe smiled, but it was sad. 'I never saw it again after the crash. It was dealt with by lawyers and the state. They offered to let me go back and get my things, but I couldn't bear to… Everything was put in storage for me, but I've never visited the storage unit.' She shrugged and looked down. 'I'm a bit of a coward.'

Maks's chest felt tight. He tipped up her chin and saw her eyes were like two oceans of green and blue. 'You're not a coward, Zoe. Far from it.'

Zoe looked up at Maks. He should be the hardest person in the world to talk to, but things that she never spoke of to anyone tripped off her tongue with an ease that shocked her.

He threw back the rest of his aperitif and said, 'Come on, let's go.'

Go where?

Zoe didn't even want to ask, not wanting to burst the incredible bubble of being with this man in this beautiful place. She felt like a miser, wanting to hoard every tiny moment.

After turning a dizzying number of corners they emerged into a small quiet square with a large ornate church at one end. Maks was leading her through to another street when she heard it. The sound of singing.

Zoe stopped. She walked over to have a closer look. Posters advertised an opera, due to take place the following evening. The singing was more audible now, coming from inside, and she looked at Maks, who shrugged and followed her into the dark interior.

People were up on a stage in costume, but no make-up. She whispered to Maks, 'It must be the dress re-hearsal. Can we stay a while?'

He nodded. She was about to sit down at the back, but Maks grabbed her hand and led her up a flight of narrow winding stairs. They came out onto a balcony on the upper level that had a view of the whole church and stage.

They were rehearsing one of Zoe's favourite operas, *La Traviata.* The music swelled and washed over and through her. She was captivated. But not captivated enough to be oblivious to Maks beside her, his long legs stretched out carelessly.

The opera company stopped for a break. Zoe sighed as the echo of the music lingered in the church walls and rafters. She glanced at Maks, who was looking at her and smiling. She felt wary. 'What?'

He snaked a hand to the back of her neck and tugged her towards him. 'You constantly surprise me. They'll be coming here tomorrow in ballgowns and tuxedoes, but I think you prefer this, don't you?'

He saw her. Damn him.

She nodded. He pulled her closer and pressed his mouth to hers. The fire ignited instantly. Voraciously. It was only a discreet but forceful cough that made them pull apart.

A priest was standing in the aisle below the balcony, looking up. Zoe went puce. Maks raised a hand to in-dicate that they were leaving. When they got outside, Zoe broke into a fit of giggles. Maks caught her, and her giggles stopped abruptly when he kissed her again, stealing her sanity. *Stealing her soul.*

He stopped the kiss. 'Let's go back to the hotel.'

Zoe nodded. She couldn't speak.

He led her down to the canal and they took a gondola. As they entered the Grand Canal from a smaller one the sun was setting behind the huge *palazzos* and bathing everything in a rosy golden light.

It was so beautiful that Zoe's breath caught. She lifted her camera, even though she knew that to try and capture it would fail miserably. But she needed to have some record of this moment, even if it would be infinitely inferior. Because she knew it wouldn't happen again.

When they arrived back at the hotel Maks barely acknowledged the manager who leapt to attention. Zoe shot him an apologetic smile as Maks pulled her into the elevator with indecent haste.

As soon as they got to the suite he closed the door and looked at Zoe. For a charged moment neither one moved. Zoe had no idea who moved first, but she was in Maks's arms, her legs wrapped around his waist, her mouth on every bit of exposed skin she could find as he walked them into the massive bedroom.

The French doors were open, and the curtains moved gently in the warm evening air, but Zoe was oblivious to everything but the spectacle of Maks's body being revealed, inch by delicious inch, as he stripped off his clothes until he was naked.

'Now you...'

He started undoing her shirt, pushing it open, pulling the lace cups of her bra down so he could cup her breasts and push her nipples into pouting peaks, begging for his hot mouth. Zoe clasped his head in her hands as his wicked mouth tended to her sensitive flesh, his hot tongue leaving a trail of fire.

Her shirt and bra were dispensed with. Shoes kicked off. Trousers opened and pulled down. Underwear ripped. She didn't care. She just craved contact. Mutual desperation fuelled their movements, and they took a simultaneous breath of relief when Maks entered her on a smooth thrust.

But the relief was soon replaced with urgency as the tension built and built, until Zoe was begging incoherently for Maks to release them both… And even though she'd been begging for it, when it came she still wasn't ready.

She was tossed high, and then fell deep down into a whirlpool of pleasure so intense that she couldn't breathe. Couldn't speak. Could only hold on as the storm racked Maks's body too and only then the tumult subsided.

Maks slumped over her body, still embedded deeply, and Zoe wrapped her legs around him and wished that this moment would never end.

When Maks woke, the bedroom was filled with the pearlescent light of dawn. He felt drunk, but it wasn't from alcohol. It was from an overload of sensual pleasure. Zoe lay curled into his side, one arm thrown over his chest and one leg over his thigh, her foot locked behind his knee, as if to stop him from going anywhere.

He extricated himself carefully from her embrace, the nerve-ends in his body firing to life as he touched the plump curve of one breast and felt the indentation of her waist...one silky thigh.

She curled up on her side, saying something in her sleep. Maks pulled a sheet over her. She was adorably slow to get going in the morning, sleepy and sexy.

Naked, he went to the open window and stood there for a moment, relishing the cool morning breeze on his overheated skin. He felt utterly sated, and yet a delicious tendril of anticipation coiled in his gut.

He heard movement behind him and looked around, a smile curving his mouth, his blood already heating at the thought of waking Zoe up in a very explicit—

Click. She was sitting up in bed and she had her camera lifted to her face. She was taking pictures.

At first Maks's smile stayed in place. 'What are you doing?'

Click. It was as if the sound of the shutter woke him from a trance. He was naked. She was taking pictures.

His smile faded. He said it again. 'What are you doing?'

Zoe lowered the camera. Not even her bare breasts could distract Maks from the sudden cold rush of reality. And the feeling of intense exposure.

'I woke up and you looked so beautiful in the light... I just... I didn't think...'

Maks shook his head. 'Don't do that.'

She put the camera down in her lap. Her eyes were wide. 'Maks, I'm sorry. I wasn't thinking. You looked so beautiful in the light... I just acted on instinct.'

A sense of vulnerability prickled over his skin. A sense of waking out of a deep dream. He felt cold, all of a sudden. He needed to get away from Zoe's huge eyes.

'I'm taking a shower.'

'Maks…?'

But he didn't turn back.

He stood under the hot spray a few seconds later, but it couldn't melt the block of ice that had formed in his gut. He didn't have to look at his phone to know that it would be blowing up after he'd rescheduled a whole day of meetings yesterday.

His brother Nikos had been renowned for this kind of behaviour—going AWOL and then turning up in the tabloids, falling out of a club with two women on his arm, in a different city to the one where he'd been due to attend meetings.

Sharif was a little more circumspect, but recently he'd been at the mercy of some unfavourable kiss-and-tells after one of too many discarded lovers had had enough.

Maks did not do this. Maks had had a well-honed instinct to keep out of the limelight after his parents' toxicity had blighted his and his sister's lives. He'd always been the solid brother. The one who never failed to turn up to meetings and was discreet in all matters.

He knew he and Zoe would be all over the papers by now, because they'd been seen together at more than one event. And if he wasn't mistaken he was pretty sure a paparazzo had been following them yesterday. He hadn't even cared all that much.

And yet it had taken *her* lifting a camera to her face to wake him up. He hadn't been able to see her face. He'd only seen that lens. It had made him realise just how far under his skin he'd let her burrow.

All the way.

No. Maks rejected that thought as he stepped out of the shower. He slung a towel around his hips and saw his face in the mirror over the sink.

What was he doing? Letting a woman get under his skin like this? When there was no way it was going to last?

The most important person in the world to Maks was Sasha, his sister. As soon as he'd been old enough he'd taken Sasha out of his father's house and had become her guardian. His father had died soon after, and anyway he hadn't even noticed that his daughter was gone from his care. Because she hadn't even been his.

Their experiences had fostered an unspoken agreement between them never to repeat the mistakes of their parents.

What he felt here, now, with Zoe, was some kind of lust-induced craziness. He knew better than this. He knew not to send mixed messages. And that was exactly what he was doing. Telling her one thing but behaving in the completely opposite way. When he thought of the previous day, wandering around Venice, hand in hand, taking a gondola—which no self-respecting Italian would *ever* do—he cringed.

Maks and his sister had been the flotsam and jetsam in the wreckage of their parents' toxic marriage, and while Sasha had no interest in the Marchetti Group, Maks did. He'd made it his priority to ensure that he helped to build a legacy that would prove to be far more stable and durable and lasting than any marriage.

That was what mattered. Not the illusion of something that didn't exist.

He knew this was an unprecedented situation. He'd

never wanted a woman for longer than a couple of dates. So it would be hard to do what he had to. But he would do it because he couldn't offer Zoe anything more.

Zoe sat on the bed for a long moment after Maks disappeared into the bathroom. She didn't have to be a genius to figure out that something seismic had just happened.

She shouldn't have taken those pictures.

But when she'd woken and seen him standing by the gently fluttering drapes she'd wondered if she was dreaming. Not awake at all. He'd looked like a living sculpture of a Greek god. Every line of his body perfectly proportioned and muscled in the light of dawn, bathing him in a kind of golden celestial glow.

Zoe had had only one impulse—to capture his beauty. She'd barely been aware of reaching for her camera and lifting it to her face. Much like the first time she'd taken his photo.

Realising that she was sitting in some kind of a stupor, waiting for him to emerge, she scrambled out of bed and took some clothes with her, washing and changing in the suite's other bathroom.

When she was drying herself afterwards she was aware of a tension she hadn't felt in days. She'd become so engrossed in Maks's world. In his masterful seduction. To the point where she'd almost forgotten that a far grittier world existed for her outside of all this...fantasy.

She'd almost forgotten that this wasn't normal. When she'd woken at first, before she'd opened her eyes and seen Maks in all his naked glory, she'd been feeling such a sense of contentment. And peace and safety.

A brief fantastical illusion.

Hard to forget, though, when the after-effects of Maks's body moving over hers, in hers, still lingered.

A cold finger traced down her spine. She hadn't felt that sense of happiness or safety in a long time—not since before her world had been torn apart and she'd lost everything she'd loved and known.

She heard Maks's voice in the suite, low. Her pulse throbbed in reaction even as she realised that this was her wake-up call. She'd allowed no one close enough to hurt her—not even Dean, who she'd *known* and believed she trusted.

She threw on some clothes, a knot in her belly at the thought of facing Maks. But for a moment, before she walked into the main room of the suite, she was gripped by a fantasy.

Maybe she was being paranoid. Skittish. Maybe Maks wasn't really that annoyed about the photos and maybe he was even now making arrangements to reschedule his work so they could spend another day together... And maybe she was safe. Maybe he hadn't got so close that he would burn her alive.

But when she entered the main room and saw Maks pacing back and forth, his cell phone clamped to his ear, dressed in a three-piece suit, she knew something had broken.

He was remote, barely glancing at her. Speaking Italian. He gestured to where breakfast was laid out on the table. Fresh coffee, pastries, fruit, cereal. But Zoe wasn't hungry.

Newspapers. Something caught her eye in one paper and she picked it up, her blood running cold. There was a picture of her and Maks at the ballet in St Petersburg.

And another of them at the fashion event. And one from yesterday, here in Venice. She was holding his hand and looking up at him, smiling. No, laughing.

Zoe sank down into a chair. She felt sick to see herself plastered across the newspapers. But she'd been incredibly naive not to expect this. She recalled seeing those pictures of Maks's brother's new wife—Maggie?—in the papers. She'd had a similar deer-in-the-headlights look.

Maks terminated his conversation. Zoe looked at him. He had a stern expression on his face. One she hadn't seen for some time.

She put down the paper. 'Is everything okay?'

Maks put his phone in his pocket. 'Not exactly, no.'

Zoe stood up again, trepidation prickling over her skin. 'What is it? Did something happen?'

Maks ran a hand through his hair, making it messy. Which only made him look sexier.

He gestured to the papers. 'I should have warned you what might happen.'

Zoe looked down again. 'It's a bit of a shock to see myself in a national newspaper…but it's not the end of the world, is it?'

'Of course it's not. But it won't happen again.'

Zoe looked at Maks. He stood only a few feet away, but he couldn't have been more remote. The little fantasy she'd entertained that he might be rearranging his day so they could spend time together mocked her now.

'What do you mean?'

Maks's grey gaze looked silver in the light. Impenetrable.

'What I mean is that this ends here and now, Zoe. It's

not fair to string it out…generating more pictures and headlines…for what? The sake of another few days? Weeks? I have to go to New York today for a meeting with my brother Sharif,' he continued. 'I can arrange for you to get back to London, or wherever you want to go.'

Something like desperation filled Zoe's gut. 'Maks, I'm sorry I took those photos. I can delete them—'

He waved a hand. 'This isn't about that. It's just… time for this to end. Like I said, I'll make sure you're taken wherever you want to go.'

Zoe felt cold. 'I can make my own way back.'

Maks said, 'You should call Pierre Gardin, the photographer from the shoot in St Petersburg. He doesn't encourage people to get in touch unless he rates them. He liked you. I know he's not a particularly pleasant person, but this is an opportunity for you to get into the business.'

Zoe was too stunned to respond straight away.

Maks looked at his watch. 'I have to go. My plane leaves within the hour. I'll leave instructions for the hotel to arrange your onward transport. Please let them take care of you, Zoe.'

He came closer, and for a second Zoe thought she saw a flash of something in his eyes, but she told herself she was imagining things. He reached out and ran a knuckle across her jaw. Her traitorous body sizzled with awareness.

'I had fun, Zoe. More fun than I've had in a long time—I won't deny it. But this was never going to go any further. I lost perspective for a short time. But better that it ends here. Now.'

Zoe's brain wouldn't work. She felt pain—incredible

pain—deep inside. The kind of pain she'd only ever felt once before. The kind of pain she'd vowed never to feel again. Yet here she was. Being eviscerated.

Her instinct was to get away as fast as possible. Curl up into a ball and push the pain back down.

He got too close. He's doing you a favour.

Somehow she managed to formulate words, to sound normal. 'I think you're right. Better for both of us to put this behind us and move on.'

Maks smiled, but it was a kind of smile she'd never seen before. Tight.

'Goodbye, Zoe.'

He walked to the door, picked up a small bag and didn't look back.

Zoe wasn't sure how long she stood there, breathless from the speed at which Maks had ruthlessly cut her out of his life.

She walked over to the balcony and marvelled at how, within twenty-four hours, this view that had felt so full of promise and wonder now felt tawdry and mocking.

She turned back into the suite. Empty. No trace left of the man who had dominated it so easily.

No, his trace was left inside her. A wound that would be added to her other wounds and which would, in time, become a scar. But not visible, like the scars on her face. Invisible.

Anger rose inside her. Anger at herself. For stepping into the blazing centre of a fire that she had *known* would consume her.

She'd already learnt a lesson at the hands of Dean

Simpson—a lesson in not letting herself be weak. How could she have let it happen again? So soon? So fatally?

Because Maks didn't make you feel weak, said an inner voice.

He'd made her feel strong. Empowered. And yet even now she could hear Maks's voice in her head, denying that he'd given her those things, those feelings. They'd been within her—all he'd done was encourage her to find them.

And he'd not held back from telling her what his life had been like. Why he had no interest in a relationship or anything more permanent. He'd been scarred too. Except, unlike Zoe, he'd not let himself get lost in a fantasy. He'd not let his innate weakness rise up to drown him. Again.

CHAPTER NINE

'ARE YOU TAKING Nikos's place in the tabloids now that he's an apparently happily settled married man?'

Sharif's tone was mocking. Maks curbed his urge to scowl at his older brother.

Downtown Manhattan was laid out all around them, visible through the huge windows, people were like industrious ants on the sidewalks. But it was wasted on Maks.

'I hardly think a couple of photos in a few tabloids is up to Nikos's standards. Or yours, I might add. You're racking up quite the tally of kiss-and-tells. Not the best judge of women who can be discreet, hmm?'

Now Sharif did scowl. Not that it marred the handsomeness of his dark good looks. 'Who is she, anyway?'

Maks bristled at his question. 'You don't need to worry about who *she* is. It's over.'

Sharif cocked an eyebrow. 'Pity. The board are still skittish, in spite of Nikos's reformation. If you were to settle down too…?'

Maks waited for the inevitable sense of rejection that usually accompanied any suggestion or notion of permanence, but all he felt was hollow. Irritation made him say, 'There's as much likelihood of that happening as of *you* getting married.'

To his surprise, Sharif didn't immediately rebut that statement. When Maks looked at him, his brother's expression was one he couldn't read. Almost…resigned.

Maks frowned. 'Sharif?'

The expression passed as if Maks had imagined it. And a familiar mocking arrogance animated his brother's face again as he said, 'That's enough gossiping, let's get on with it.'

'By all means,' Maks responded, more than happy to focus on work.

A few hours later, in his hotel suite in Manhattan, Maks nursed a whisky as he looked out over the glittering lights of the city that never slept. He felt as if *he* might never sleep again. Restless under his skin. Hungry in his blood. *For her.*

He still wanted Zoe.

He'd never wanted a woman for longer than a brief period.

A tantalising prospect struck him. Maybe he'd been too hasty? Maybe he could come to an arrangement with her in which—?

No. He ruthlessly shut down that train of thought. She wasn't that kind of woman. Sophisticated. Who knew the rules of the game. He'd been her first lover. *She'd just got under his skin.*

All he had to do was remember Zoe's reaction earlier, when he'd broken things off. The way she'd gone so pale. Her eyes huge. Stricken. It had only confirmed for him that he was doing the right thing. They had no future. As it was, he'd already dragged her into the public eye. After accusing *her* of being a paparazzi! The irony was not welcome.

But he couldn't regret seducing her—not when it had been so earth-shatteringly satisfying.

He had no right to give her any hope for more. She'd been a brief aberration. A temptation he shouldn't have succumbed to. A temptation he wouldn't succumb to again.

Three weeks later

Zoe was gritty-eyed after another broken night's sleep. Broken by dreams about Maks. And nightmares. In the latest one she'd been in Venice, endlessly wandering the narrow labyrinthine streets, searching for him, only to catch a tiny glimpse at the last second before he disappeared around another corner.

She hated herself for being so weak. He'd dumped her.

She told herself yet again that he'd done her a favour as she walked to her local corner shop for supplies.

There was nothing like being back in the grittier end of London to remind her of where she belonged. So when she looked down and saw the pictures on the front page of the tabloid newspaper she had to blink several times, wondering if she was still dreaming. Or hallucinating.

It was Maks. He was naked. He was smiling intimately at whoever was taking the picture. Drapes fluttered behind him. For a second Zoe felt as if someone had skewered her with a red-hot poker, but then she realised that these weren't different pictures. These were *her* pictures. Just after she'd taken this picture his demeanour had changed utterly. And then he'd dumped her.

She hadn't even looked back at those photos herself since that day. Not wanting to see the moment when his face had gone from dreamy and sexy to icy cold. Yet now they were plastered all over these grubby tabloids for all the world to see.

'I don't think it's a good idea, Miss Collins.'

Zoe tried not to sound as desperate as she felt, after a long day of trying to track Maks down. He'd ignored all her attempts to call or text him. But she knew he was here, at his townhouse.

'Hamish, please. I need to speak to him.'

Maks's housekeeping manager looked as if he was about to close the door in her face, but then he stood back and said tersely, 'I'll ask him. Wait here.'

Zoe stood in the hall of the stunning townhouse. It was a very different reception from the last one she'd received here. Now it couldn't be frostier.

After a long moment Hamish returned. 'He'll see you for a few minutes. Follow me.'

Relief flooded Zoe, followed quickly by trepidation. She'd been trying to get to Maks all day, but now that she was here she wasn't even sure what she would say.

Hamish led her into a room she hadn't been in before. A large study. Dark wood-panelled walls. Shelves. Modern technology. A TV on the wall with the news on mute.

And Maks. Standing behind his desk in a shirt and dark trousers. Sleeves rolled up. Hands on hips.

To see him again in close proximity almost made her stumble. She locked her legs.

The door closed behind her and Maks walked over to a drinks cabinet, pouring himself a drink. He didn't offer her one. He turned around. He looked calm, but Zoe could feel the tension.

'Why did you do it, Zoe?'

She felt sick—she'd been feeling sick all day. 'I didn't.'

He ignored her denial. 'How much did you get? If you'd offered them to me first, I might have given you more.'

A sense of desperation flooded Zoe, eclipsing the nausea. 'I didn't sell the photos, Maks, I swear. I have no idea how the papers got them.'

Maks put his glass down and perched on one corner of his desk, for all the world as if this was a civil conversation and as if she hadn't just spoken. 'I mean, I shouldn't be surprised. After all, you have form. The first time we met you were taking my picture and trespassing.'

Zoe's cheeks grew hot. 'This isn't the same.'

'No, it's not. It's worse.'

His voice was like the crack of a whip. Zoe's insides were clenched so tight she almost had a cramp.

'I know how much you hate your privacy being invaded. You know me…you know I would never do something like this.'

Maks just looked at her, no expression on his face. Those silver eyes cold as mercury.

'I thought I did. I thought you were an open book. I thought you were different. But you weren't at all. I knew you weren't happy when I broke things off,' he continued. 'But I had no idea you'd stoop so low to get back at me. Or that you were so mercenary. You had me fooled with your apparent lack of interest in anything material. Your humble but cosy flat.'

Zoe flinched inwardly. How could he think that had all been an act? But her conscience pricked hard. In a way he was right. It *wasn't* the whole truth of her existence. But Maks would never want to hear about that. Not now.

All she could say was, 'I didn't do this.'

Maks stood up straight, folded his arms. 'Stop with the lies, Zoe. They make fools of both of us. We know the money went into an account in a bank right beside where you live.'

Zoe stared at Maks, absorbing his words. Shock, dismay and confusion made her head throb. Who could have done this to her? To him?

Maks's arms were locked so tight across his chest that Zoe could see his biceps bulging under the thin material of his shirt. The blood quickened in her veins. Even now, in the midst of all of this, when he was looking at her as if he wanted to—

His lip curled. 'Take the grubby money that you got from the papers and get out. You won't get anything more from me, so if that's why you came it's a wasted journey.'

'Maks, I swear. I didn't—' But she stopped talking. Maks was a cold, remote statue. Not interested. Convinced of her guilt.

She felt incredible hurt that he could be so quick to misjudge her.

'Get out,' he said. 'I never want to see you again.'

Something cracked apart inside her, breaking into a thousand pieces. She'd thought she'd protected herself so well, but she hadn't protected herself at all.

It took a few seconds for the red haze to fade enough in Maks's head for him to realise that Zoe had left. For a stomach-plummeting second he thought he might have actually imagined that she'd come here, that she'd stood in front of him protesting her innocence. Hair down. Those scars visible against her pale skin. Her eyes as big as he remembered. Her mouth as lush. *As tempting.*

No.

He unlocked his arms from his chest and unclenched his jaw. She *had* been here. He could smell her scent in the air and had to resist the urge to breathe it deep.

He picked up his glass and drained it in one gulp. He didn't even wince as it flamed down his throat. He barely felt it. His fingers gripped the heavy crystal so tightly he had to relax them for fear of cracking it.

His skin still crawled when he thought of the look on his executive assistant's face that morning when he'd arrived at the Marchetti offices shortly after dawn—and the fact that he hadn't been sleeping well for the past few weeks was *not* something he wanted to associate with the women who had just left.

His assistant hadn't been able to meet his eyes as he'd cleared his throat and said, 'Have you seen the papers yet, sir?'

Maks, feeling irritable, had replied, 'No. Why?'

'There's something you should see.'

His assistant had laid out a sheaf of the main tabloids on his desk and it had taken Maks a moment even to understand what he was looking at. *Himself. Naked.*

His first reaction hadn't even been anger. Or shock. It had been to remember that morning, with the sun coming up on the Grand Canal in Venice, the breeze cooling his overheated body. The sense of contentment and sensual satisfaction that had oozed through him. Along with that delicious pique of anticipation.

The picture in the papers had captured that moment when he'd looked around and caught Zoe with her camera raised to her face. He'd smiled. Not minding in that first instance that she was taking his picture. And then reality had hit like a bucket of cold water. He'd realised just how lax he'd been. How blinded by lust. To let someone get that close! Close enough to steal his very soul.

The thing that burned and roiled in Maks's gut most was that a lifetime of cynicism had let him down. He never would have suspected Zoe of having the kind of wherewithal to do something like this, and yet up until he'd met her he would have assumed anyone was capable of anything. No matter how innocent they looked or acted.

He thought of all the little moments when he'd doubted she could really be that gauche, that innocent. Naive. No, not naive. Unjaded.

For all he knew she could have faked her virginity— she'd told him beforehand, so of course that would have made him less likely to question if she really was or not. He knew what good actors women were; he'd seen his mother lie over and over again about her numerous affairs until she hadn't cared any more and had freely admitted to them, to taunt his father.

That was when he'd hit her.

They'd divorced soon after that.

But maybe even worse than all that was the fact that when he'd woken today, after weeks of sleepless nights and sexual frustration eating him up inside, he'd been seriously tempted to get in touch with Zoe again.

And say what? He hadn't even been sure, but he'd just wanted her. Badly.

He could blame her for making a fool out of him all he wanted, but in the end *he* was the fool.

Two months later

Nikos clapped Maks on the back as they walked into the exclusive Marchetti Group hotel bar in Paris. 'I should have posed naked years ago. I always wanted to be named Sexiest Man of the Year—and, let's face it, I'm way sexier than you.'

Maks gritted his jaw, which seemed to be in a permanent state of grit now. 'I didn't *pose*.'

Nikos ignored him. 'You could have gone into modelling, Maks. Wasted opportunity.'

Maks opened his mouth to unleash another diatribe at Nikos, who was insufferably happy all the time now, but at that moment he saw his oldest brother, Sharif, taking a seat in a discreet corner booth. Sharif caught his eye and Maks nodded in his direction, steering Nikos towards the table.

It was a rare occurrence that they were all in Paris at

the same time, and an even rarer occurrence that they were meeting for a drink.

When they were seated around the table with their drinks, Nikos addressed the elephant in the room. 'This is serendipitous, indeed—all the brothers around a table that isn't twelve foot long and full of other board members. Something to tell us, Sharif?'

Their eldest brother looked as unreadable and unflappable as ever. 'Can't we at least pretend we're a normal family?' His tone was mocking.

Maks let out a spontaneous snort of laughter. 'Normal? What's that? None of us can lay claim to knowing the first thing about what it's like to be normal.' That was followed by a far too familiar sense of hollowness in his gut.

Nikos said, 'Speak for yourselves. I'm a happily committed married father of nearly two children.'

Nikos's wife was pregnant with their second child. It had just been announced in the press.

Sharif said darkly, 'We'll see how long that lasts.'

Maks felt Nikos bristle beside him. He put a hand on his arm. 'He's just jealous.'

Now Sharif made a snorting noise.

They all took a sip of their drinks, tension bubbling under the surface, but it was tempered by something far more tenuous and delicate. *New.*

Maks realised that, as much as they might be wary of each other, they respected each other at least.

Then Sharif, sounding uncharacteristically *un*-mocking said, 'Actually, I wanted to let you know that the group has seen the best returns in a decade. And that's down to us all.' He looked at Nikos. 'The news of your marriage and fatherhood has stabilised nervy share-holders.'

Nikos grinned, lifting his glass. 'Happy to help in any small way I can.'

Sharif went on, glancing from Nikos to Maks. 'I know we all have our reasons for investing our time and effort into this company, and that none of us had to accept this inheritance. God knows, our father didn't inspire loyalty in any of us, but I'm glad we're in this together. I think we can take the Marchetti Group above and beyond anything our father ever imagined, and in doing so we can forge a new beginning.'

Nikos frowned. 'That almost sounds like you've got something planned, brother.'

Sharif shrugged, but Maks noticed that he was watching them carefully. He said, 'I'm just saying that there is no limit to what we can achieve now we're united.'

At that moment Nikos's phone buzzed. It was on the table, and Maks saw an image of Maggie's smiling face and their son Daniel's, close to hers. Daniel was grinning cherubically, with the dark hair and eyes of his father.

Nikos picked up the phone, looking at his brothers. 'Are we done here, or do you want to sit and braid each other's hair some more?'

Sharif rolled his eyes, but his mouth twitched. 'No, go—play happy families. Enjoy it while it lasts.'

Nikos was already up, answering his phone with a sexy growl. '*Moro mou,* you were meant to call me an hour ago…'

Maks knew Maggie well enough by now to know

that she'd probably be rolling her eyes at her husband, and a curious little ache formed in his chest at the thought of Nikos and his growing family unit. At his very obvious adoration for his wife. It was such an alien thing to witness.

All of sudden Maks realised that in spite of everything he didn't share Sharif's cynicism. He had a sense that whatever Nikos and Maggie had, it was very real.

Sharif's phone rang. He answered it and went still. Then he said, 'I'm making the most of a set of circumstances set down many years ago. It'll be in all of our interests to take advantage of this opportunity. Let them know I'll expect things to happen within the next couple of months.'

Maks looked at Sharif when he had terminated his call. 'That was cryptic. Anything you want to share?'

Sharif fixed his dark gaze on Maks. For a moment Maks had the impression that Sharif wanted to share something but all he did say was, 'It's nothing that concerns you. Stay in touch, brother. And forewarn me next time you decide to pose naked for the papers. It was rather more of my little brother than I cared to see over my breakfast.'

Sharif got up to leave and Maks rose too, gritting his jaw again. 'I didn't *pose*.'

But Sharif was already striding out of the bar, with a couple of assistants who'd been hiding in a corner chasing after him.

Feeling irrationally irritable and irritated, Maks moved to a stool at the bar, ordering a drink. He noticed a few women on their own. One met his eyes. She was beautiful. Willowy, blonde. Confident. Exactly the kind of woman whose clear invitation he would have accepted before. Except he felt nothing. No stirring of interest. *Nada*. Zilch.

He turned to his drink. His libido only seemed to come to life at night now. When he woke sweaty and aching all over after explicitly sexual dreams featuring a treacherous liar and a thief—

'Maks, you dark horse! Are congratulations in order?'

Maks looked up and to his side, to see the smirking face of photographer Pierre Gardin. Another reminder of Zoe that he didn't need. 'What are you talking about, Pierre?'

'Your girlfriend was working with me this week, and the rumour on set was that she's pregnant. She kept disappearing to the bathroom, but she's still the best assistant I've had in a long time. I hate to admit it, but I think she's got real potential to—'

Maks swivelled around on his stool. He could see Pierre's mouth moving but the sound was muffled. He wanted to shake the man.

He cut through whatever he was saying now. 'What did you say?'

Pierre stopped talking and cocked his head, eyes narrowing on Maks. 'Actually, Zoe never mentioned you. Maybe you're not together any more? Maybe the baby isn't yours? I can't keep up with these young people and their love affairs...'

Baby. Pregnant.

Maks was having a hard time getting his brain to absorb those words. It was so nonsensical.

And then Maks had a mental image of Zoe in bed with another man and his brain went white-hot.

'Where is she?'

Pierre frowned. 'I have no idea. She went home—back to London, presumably.'

Maks's brain was melting.

Pregnant.

Yet she hadn't called him.

Do you blame her? asked a caustic voice. The words he'd last thrown at her reverberated in his head: *Get out. I never want to see you again.*

Was he even the father?

'Maks, are you okay?'

No. He wasn't. For weeks now he'd been avoiding thinking about Zoe's stricken face when she'd come to his townhouse that night, and her entreaty, *'You know I'd never do something like this.'* Avoiding the niggling question as to why she would have come to his house if she'd really leaked the photos and been paid for them. Surely that wasn't the action of a guilty person? Surely she would have just disappeared with the money?

His conscience pricked. His team had offered to look deeper into the leak of the photos. To confirm beyond doubt that it had been Zoe. But Maks had stopped them, telling himself that he *knew.*

But now he wasn't so sure at all.

Within twenty-four hours Maks was standing outside Zoe's door. Not used to waiting for much, if anything, he had to curb his impatience as she seemed to take an age to open it.

When she did, and he saw the shock on her face and the way her eyes widened, he couldn't stop the rush of blood and instant jolt of lust.

He still wanted her.

As if he hadn't already known that.

'Why didn't you answer my texts or calls?' His helpless reaction made his voice harsher than he'd intended.

She pulled an over-large shapeless cardigan tighter around her. Maks looked down. He couldn't see any visible signs of pregnancy, but she did look pale.

'Maks. What are you doing here?'

He moved into the apartment and shut the door behind him.

'We need to talk.'

She didn't look so shocked now. She moved back. 'You said you never wanted to see me again.'

'That was before…'

'Before what?'

Suddenly Maks was reluctant to ask if she was pregnant, not ready to have that conversation yet, so instead he said, 'Did you sell the photos, Zoe?'

'I told you I didn't, but you refused to listen to me.'

'I'm listening now.'

Zoe said nothing for a long moment, and then, 'You've actually saved me a phone call. I was going to ring your office today.'

'About what?'

'I know who did sell the photos.'

Maks frowned. 'Who?'

'I was hacked by my ex—Dean Simpson. He works in IT and my passwords wouldn't have been hard to crack. I upload all my pictures to an online storage facility. It's a reflex—something I learnt to do long ago, to make sure I don't lose work.'

Maks refused to let go of his cynicism completely. He folded his arms. 'Why would he hack you?'

Zoe paced away to the window. She looked very slight under the voluminous cardigan and in her loose pyjama pants.

She turned around. 'He must have seen the pictures of us and acted out of spite and jealousy. I didn't tell you everything about him—about why he…attacked me.'

A sense of unease prickled over Maks's skin. 'Tell me now.'

She faced him properly. Her scars stood out against her pale skin. 'The reason we broke up was not just because he wanted an intimacy that I realised I didn't want. It was because he wanted something else from me. He hadn't looked me up in London just because he happened to be here—he'd targeted me.'

'Why would he target you?'

For a long moment she said nothing, and then, 'Because he found out who I was and what that meant.'

Maks frowned. 'What are you talking about? Who *are* you?'

Zoe started to pace back and forth. Maks tried not to let his gaze drop to where the vee of her T-shirt dipped low enough to reveal a hint of breast. Even that tiny hint of provocation had heated blood rushing to his groin.

'Zoe,' he snapped, in response to her effect on him. 'I don't have all day for this.'

She looked at him, eyes huge. He saw her jaw set.

'I didn't ask you to come here. If you have more important things to be doing then by all means leave.'

Maks forced his blood to cool. 'Go on.'

She took an audible breath. 'I didn't tell you who

my parents were. My father was Stephen Collins, the photographer and author, and my mother was Simone Bryant, the heiress.'

Maks shook his head as if that might clear it, trying to better assimilate this information. He knew her father's name—anyone with even a passing interest in news and current affairs would have heard of Stephen Collins, the world-renowned photojournalist who'd covered some of the grisliest wars. And Simone Bryant had famously been the last remaining heiress to a vast fortune built from one of Ireland's oldest breweries. Maks had a vague memory of a golden society couple...

He focused on Zoe again. 'You lied to me about who you are.'

Zoe bristled visibly. 'I didn't lie. I just didn't tell you exactly who I am. Collins is a common name...'

'Your father won a Pulitzer prize for his non-fiction and then he became a bestselling crime author. I have his books on my shelves.' He stopped, recalling how Zoe had been looking at the books on his shelves in London. She'd probably been laughing at him the whole time. *Dio.* 'Why the hell would you hide who your parents were?'

Maks looked at her as if seeing her for the first time. He felt ridiculously betrayed that Zoe had kept this information from him. But he could also see now where her talent came from. She had it in spades. It was evident in every picture hanging on the walls of this tiny flat.

She just looked at him with those huge eyes.

Maks frowned as something else sank in. 'Your parents were wealthy.'

Zoe nodded. 'Very. When they died, my inheritance was kept in trust for me till I turned eighteen.'

Maks looked around. 'And yet you live like an impoverished student.'

'Because I never wanted to touch that money.'

He was taken aback at the stark tone in her voice. 'Why not?'

Zoe's throat moved as if she was struggling to say the words. 'Because it was blood money. Money that I never should have had. I got it at the expense of my parents' deaths. My brother, who never got to live his life. Of course I wasn't going to use it. I've given most of it away to charity.'

Maks felt a pain near his chest as he thought of the fact that Zoe blamed herself for the accident. He pushed it down.

'What has Dean Simpson got to do with any of this?'

Zoe sighed. 'When I was eighteen I left Ireland for London. I'd always wanted to follow in my father's footsteps, and he started his photography career here. Also, there was nothing for me in Dublin. No family. No ties. Just grief and bittersweet memories.'

Maks was still reeling from all this information and what it meant about the woman in front of him. *If* what she was saying was true.

He said, 'Go on.'

She looked at him. 'I never expected to see Dean Simpson again. When he came to London and tracked me down I realised I was lonely. I trusted him. We'd been in the same foster home. He was my first boyfriend. We had a shared past. What I didn't know was that he'd somehow found out about my background, and my inheritance, and had come to pursue a relationship with a view to getting his hands on it. When Dean brought it up I was shocked. I told him what I've told you—that I wanted nothing to do with the money, that I'd given most of it away to charity—and that was when Dean got angry with me…when he realised I'd been getting rid of it.'

Zoe lifted her chin.

'If you don't believe me you can check the bank account where the money from the pictures was lodged. It's in Dean's name. He didn't even try very hard to cover his tracks.'

Maks looked at Zoe, a small obstinately cynical part of him refusing to give in to what his gut was telling him—that she was innocent. Always had been. In more ways than one.

'How do I know you weren't working together? That you haven't spent your entire inheritance and you're looking to make more money at my expense?'

Zoe went so pale that for a moment Maks thought she might faint. Instead, she stalked past him and went to the door, opening it.

She looked at him. 'Get out, Maks.'

A lead weight seemed to be stuck in his gut. And then he remembered. The reason why he'd come here in the first place.

He said, 'There's something else. I bumped into Pierre Gardin. He told me that you might be pregnant. Is it true?'

Zoe looked at Maks. She forced herself to breathe, to let oxygen get to her brain. Anger, betrayal, and so many other emotions roiled in her gut that she felt light-headed. All mixed up with a clawing need to throw herself into Maks's arms and wind herself around him like a vine.

She forced all that out. The urge to self-protect was paramount.

When she felt as if she could sound calm she said, 'That's the most ridiculous thing I ever heard.'

'Pierre said you weren't well.'

Zoe's face grew warm and she avoided Maks's eye. 'I had a bug, that was all.'

'So you're not pregnant?'

She gripped the handle of the door. 'Please leave, Maks. I have an English class to teach today and I'm already late.'

Maks sounded frustrated. 'Zoe…if you are, you need to tell me.'

She finally looked at him, focusing on anger to block out all the other disturbing emotions. 'Why? When I know exactly how you feel about having a family? You're the last man I'd choose to be the father of my child.'

'If you were pregnant with my baby I would take responsibility. You wouldn't be alone.'

The thought of Maks having to *take responsibility* for her made bile rise inside Zoe. She said, 'Even if I was pregnant I wouldn't come to you, because I don't need to. No matter how much money I give to charity, the interest alone on what's left keeps me rich beyond anything I know what to do with. So *if* I was pregnant, which I'm not, I wouldn't need you anyway.'

CHAPTER TEN

PLEASE LEAVE, ZOE begged silently, just wanting to escape Maks's far too probing eyes. Relief moved through her when he finally walked to the door and stepped over the threshold.

He turned around. Grim. 'If what you say is true then I owe you an apology. Simpson victimised you as much as me.'

Hurt gripped her again at his reluctance to trust her. 'You don't owe me anything.'

Zoe shut the door and stood in a stupor for a long moment, staring at her closed door. She heard the sound of the main door closing heavily. The throttle of a powerful engine.

In spite of her brave words just now, she knew it wasn't the last she'd see of Maks. Not by a long shot. Not just because he might come back to apologise, as his integrity would demand. But for another far more pressing reason.

Her hand went to her belly. She'd lied. Unforgivably. Blatantly. She *was* pregnant and her little bump was growing every day. But the shock of having Maks here in her space, confronting her, suggesting she might have been colluding with Dean Simpson, had decimated any urge she might have had to tell him today.

Of course she would tell him she was pregnant. When she could do so on her terms. When she could prepare herself for the inevitable distaste she'd see on his face. When she would be able to stand in front of him and tell him calmly and rationally that she was prepared to do this on her own and didn't expect him to *take responsibility*.

Terrified, but filled with a sense of focus and a determination to get over her fear of loss and grief, she knew she owed it to her baby to do her best to try. To create a secure life for them both. To shield them from the fear she would feel every day.

It was time to reassess her experiences and do things differently. She had a child to support now. She couldn't continue like an out-of-work student, skirting around the edges of life, ignoring the fact that she had the means to live well. It wasn't just about her and her guilt any more.

Maks felt sick. It had taken the most rudimentary of internet searches to find the news reports on the tragic crash that had killed Zoe's family. Leaving her the sole survivor. There'd been pictures of the car wreckage that had made him feel weak, and pictures of Zoe, taken before the crash.

Her father had been tall and dashingly handsome, her mother blonde and beautiful. Like Zoe. There'd been pictures of a three-year-old Zoe holding her baby brother, grinning proudly. And a lot of breathless speculation about the young, tragically orphaned heiress.

It also hadn't been hard to find the philanthropic foundation she'd set up to donate money anonymously to various charities. Set up—Maks suspected—on her eighteenth birthday.

He recalled how she'd sounded almost bewildered when she'd mentioned the fact that no matter what she did the interest kept growing on her remaining inheritance. He'd never met anyone before who'd actively tried to get rid of money.

The way she'd denied herself out of a sense of guilt and grief made Maks's chest feel tight.

A knock sounded on his home office door. Hamish stuck his head around it. 'Lunch, boss?'

Maks didn't feel hungry. He stood up. 'No. Can you get my assistant to meet me here? And call my legal team. I have some information for them.'

'Sure thing.'

Hamish left and Maks walked over to the window, looking out unseeingly. Zoe wasn't pregnant. And even if she was, as she'd pointed out, she didn't actually need his support.

He should be feeling relieved. She was right. A family was the last thing he'd ever wanted. A baby. No matter what kind of ache he might have felt when he'd thought of his brother Nikos and his family. An ache that was still there now.

He'd misjudged Zoe badly. And any sense of betrayal that she hadn't told him about her family was fading fast. He could understand why.

A mixture of complicated emotions roiled in his gut. He didn't usually judge people out of hand. He was actually far less likely to jump to conclusions than either of his brothers. But with Zoe... She'd pushed his buttons from the moment he'd first seen her. And at the first sign of an opportunity to believe the worst about her he'd jumped at it.

The worst thing was, he knew exactly why he'd reacted like that. Because he hadn't been prepared to admit that he still wanted her. That he wasn't ready to let her go. And more. Much more.

Zoe stood on the stony beach and looked out at the Irish Sea. It was a blustery day with leaden skies. Typical Irish weather. She turned around and looked up to the cliff behind her, where a distinctive yellow house stood out. That had been her home. The family home where she'd felt loved and safe and as if nothing could touch her.

A deep sigh moved through her as the wind whipped her hair around her face.

She'd spent the last few days in a storage facility, going through her family's possessions, and she felt wrung out but also a little lighter. As if a weight was finally lifting off her shoulders.

She faced the sea again and tried to ignore the dull pain that dogged her every step. *Maks*. Every time she thought about him she forced her mind away again. But, like a well-worn groove, her mind kept going over all the reasons why she was so reluctant to contact him and reveal the truth about her pregnancy: he'd never promised her anything but a finite affair; he believed that she'd betrayed his trust, which just confirmed how little he'd really thought of her; he didn't want a relationship or a child or a family.

And, even more damningly, she now knew why he'd appeared on her doorstep in London.

He hadn't really wanted to verify her guilt or innocence. He'd been there to see if she was pregnant. Because the last thing he wanted was more adverse publicity.

She cursed herself again for letting him close enough to hurt her. *Devastate her. Fatally.*

No, she told herself now. Not fatal. She was still here. Whole. *Pregnant.*

She would have to tell him sooner or later and deal with the fact that he would be in her life in some capacity for ever…but not today.

Zoe turned around to walk away from the sea, back up towards the hotel where she was staying while she went through her family's things.

She'd only taken a few steps into the lobby when she heard her name being called.

'Zoe.'

She stopped. The voice was deep. Hypnotic. She didn't want to turn around. *It couldn't be.* And yet no one knew her here.

She turned around. Maks was standing a few feet away in dark clothes. He'd never looked more beautiful or sexy.

Zoe felt weak. 'What are you doing here? How did you know where I was?'

Maks took a step towards her. She stepped back—a self-protective reflex. She saw his jaw clench and felt ridiculously like apologising.

'I went to your flat in London. Your neighbour told

me you'd moved out and that you were taking a trip to Dublin. It wasn't hard to track you down.'

Not for a billionaire with means at his disposal, Zoe thought to herself. She could feel herself responding to his proximity. She wanted to drink him in. She wanted to reach up and pull his head down and feel that hard mouth on hers. Every part of her body tingled with awareness and she vaguely wondered if it had anything to do with being pregnant.

Pregnant.

She wasn't ready. Not today.

Coward.

Feeling desperate, she asked, 'Why are you here, Maks? I thought we'd said all we had to say.'

'Can we go somewhere more private?'

Zoe looked around. People were practically tripping over themselves when they saw Maks Marchetti in this very mediocre hotel lobby. Zoe felt like rolling her eyes. He literally was too beautiful to be out in public without causing an incident.

'You have a room here?'

Zoe's mind seized at the thought of him in her small suite. But there was nowhere else private and, as much as she didn't want to tell him about the pregnancy, she knew she had to.

Reluctantly she walked over to the elevator, without waiting to see if he followed her. But she could feel him behind her. Tall. Powerful. His scent was exotic. Musky. *Sexy.*

The tension crackled between them when they were in the elevator—so much that Zoe got an electric shock when she pushed the button for her floor. It was a relief to get out and walk down the short corridor to her room.

She went in and immediately went over to the window, crossing her arms, looking at Maks warily as he followed her in. She noticed more now. His hair was longer. Jaw stubbled. He looked tired. Dishevelled.

Her heart squeezed with an unbidden urge to know if he was okay. And then she lambasted herself for being weak. She hated him. His betrayal of her was far worse than anything she'd unwittingly done to him.

But when he looked at her she could feel herself aligning towards him. Her head and body at war. She was melting. Aching.

She didn't hate him at all.

'Maks, what do you want?' Her voice was sharp. Panicked.

You. Maks just restrained himself from saying it. Seeing Zoe up close again made him feel primal. Her lithe petite form. That honey-blonde hair, wild and messy from the wind. Cheeks pink. Eyes like two stormy oceans.

He forced his brain out of his pants. 'I came to say I'm sorry. I should have given you the benefit of the doubt. I knew you better than that.'

The pink faded from her cheeks. She looked pale now.

'You've got proof that Dean hacked into my account and sold the pictures.' Her voice was flat.

'No, I didn't need to. I should have trusted you. I gave his name to the authorities. They informed me that he was picked up in Spain yesterday, and he's admitted everything. They're extraditing him back to Ireland to face charges. I won't hold back from bringing the full force of the law down on him, Zoe.'

'Oh.'

It shouldn't surprise Maks that Zoe looked troubled at that news. She probably felt sorry for her ex.

She said, 'You didn't have to come all the way here to tell me that, but thank you.'

He nodded. 'Yes, I did. The first time I saw you I accused you of being something you weren't. You…you have an effect on me. Normally I can be rational, but with you…that goes out the window.'

Zoe bit her lip. 'I can't help that.'

Now she sounded injured. Maks cursed himself. Shook his head.

'You got too close, Zoe. Closer than I've ever let anyone get. The only other person who knows me as well is my sister. That's why I let you go in Venice. When you took my picture, and when it didn't immediately feel like a violation…it was like a wake-up call. I panicked.'

His forced out words through the weight in his gut.

'And then, when the pictures came out, I jumped on any excuse to damn you…so I wouldn't have to acknowledge how much you'd got to me. How much I wanted you. How much I still want you now. Pushing you away was easier than being honest with myself.'

Zoe's eyes went wide, colour flooding her cheeks. He could see the pulse at her throat beating hectically.

'I don't… I don't want you any more,' she said.

He moved closer. Unable not to. Zoe looked at him as if in a trance. 'Don't lie, Zoe.'

She moved back. 'So what if I do still want you? You dumped me, remember?'

Maks stopped right in front of her. Her scent, fresh and sweet, wound around him. He smelled the sea too. Salty. Something in him calmed for the first time in weeks.

'Maybe that was a mistake.'

She'd been looking at his mouth. Now her eyes met his.

'What's that supposed to mean? What do you want from me?'

All Maks knew was that what he really wanted was too huge and terrifying to articulate. Far easier to focus on the hunger that had been eating him up for weeks.

He reached out, put his hands on her arms. He felt the tension in her body even as she swayed towards him.

'I want *you*. We both want this. We can talk later, hmm…?'

Zoe was drowning in a sea of rising lust. The urge to just sink into Maks, allow him to seduce her again, was overwhelming. She desperately wanted to forget everything for a moment…forget the need to think about what he'd said, about what it might mean.

She wasn't sure what signal of acquiescence she gave, but Maks was tugging her towards him and saying, 'Are you sure?'

Zoe just nodded, her eyes fixed on his mouth, silently begging him to kiss her. And then he was, and for the first time in months she felt as if she could breathe again.

It was fast and furious. Clothes were dragged off, thrown aside. They only stopped for a moment when they were naked. Zoe touched Maks reverently, feeling emotional. She'd thought she wouldn't see him like this again.

He pulled her down onto the bed and she sank into him, her whole body melting and on fire at the same time. She gasped when his fingers explored her, testing her readiness.

He moved over her and she welcomed him into the cradle of her body, breathing deep as he moved inside her, deeper and deeper, until she couldn't breathe any more and her whole body tightened before the exquisite release.

Zoe fell down into a warm comforting blanket of peace and satisfaction, only vaguely aware of the rush of warmth inside her.

When Zoe woke a few hours later the sun had started dipping in the sky. She had her back to Maks. They touched at every point where he spooned her. Her bottom was tucked against the potency of his body—no less potent now, even in sleep.

His arm was wrapped around her, his hand splayed across her. Zoe went cold. His hand was right there… on the thickening swell of her belly.

Panic gripped her. She moved as stealthily as she could, dislodging his hand, moving out from under his arm.

He stirred and said a sleepy, 'Zoe?'

She mumbled something and fled to the bathroom on jelly legs, closing the door behind her. She looked at herself in the mirror. Her eyes were sparkling and her face was flushed. She didn't have to look further to know the evidence of Maks's touch would be all over her body.

She took in everything he'd said before they'd made love. He'd apologised. He hadn't even sought proof of Dean's guilt. He finally trusted her. *He still wanted her.*

That could be the case—and she couldn't stop the hitch of joy and relief inside her at that fact—but she had to remember what was at stake here. She was pregnant, and as soon as Maks knew that everything would change again.

Like that morning in Venice, he'd go cold. Let her go. Because he didn't want more.

She couldn't do this—not now...not when she felt so raw.

But she had no choice. She had to let him know.

She went back into the bedroom and steeled herself, not prepared for the deflation she felt to find Maks still asleep. She looked over his body greedily. She noticed that he had shadows under his eyes. As if he hadn't slept for a while. Wishful thinking that it might have anything to do with her.

She dressed quickly, quietly, wanting to be ready to face him.

Maks stirred again, and those grey eyes opened. He looked for her and found her. Came up on his elbow, smiled sleepily. Sexily. Held out his hand. 'Hey, come back here.'

Zoe teetered on the brink of blurting it all out. She had to tell him. *Now.* But in this moment before she said anything, before she ruined it with reality, a different future shimmered between them. A chance to go back into that Maks bubble, where time stopped and became magical.

Zoe wished she could go back there even as she knew

it wasn't really what she wanted. Because she'd suddenly realised here, just a couple of kilometres from her old family home, what she *did* really want. And she couldn't bear to have Maks lay it to waste. Not just yet.

Instead of blurting out what she should be saying, she said, 'I'm sorry, I can't do this. I can't just go back to what we had for as long as it might last. I want more, Maks.'

She turned before she could see his expression change and fled the room, heading blindly downstairs and back out of the hotel, down to the stony beach.

Zoe felt Maks's presence before she saw him. She was sitting on the beach, knees pulled up to her chest. He sat down beside her. She didn't look at him.

He surprised her, asking, 'Is this near where your house was?'

She nodded. 'It's the big yellow house up on the cliff behind us. This beach is where we used to come and play.'

'It's beautiful here. You were lucky.'

Zoe felt a pang to think of Maks's toxic childhood. At least she'd known happiness and love for a while.

Knowing that she couldn't delay any longer, Zoe stood up.

Maks rose fluidly beside her. She tried not to be so aware of his body.

'Maks, I—'

'There's something—'

They both looked at each other. Maks's mouth quirked. 'You first.'

'No, you—please.'

Coward, an inner voice mocked her. She pushed it down.

Maks huffed out a breath of air, ran a hand through his hair, making it stick up messily. Sexily.

'Okay. I want to say that when I came to your flat and found out you weren't pregnant I expected to be relieved. After all, having a baby is the last thing I've ever wanted. A family...'

'You told me.' And she really didn't need reminding. Not now.

'But the truth is that I wasn't relieved. What I felt was a lot more ambiguous.'

Zoe's breath stalled for a second. She looked at Maks. 'What are you saying?'

He shrugged minutely. 'Just that I realised I'd changed. Seeing Nikos with his family...seeing how happy he is...it made me realise that not all families are toxic.'

'Mine wasn't,' Zoe said, almost to herself. 'My mother and father adored each other—and us...'

It had been so perfect and she realised now that a part of her had always afraid she'd never attain that level of perfection, more than she was ever afraid of loss or grief. If she was brutally being honest with herself.

Maks continued. 'It made me realise that perhaps a baby wouldn't be the worst thing in the world...'

Zoe stumbled backwards so abruptly that Maks reached out as if to steady her. She ducked out of his reach, dreading him touching her for fear he'd see his effect on her.

'Why would you say this now?'

Dear God. Did he know? Could he tell? He'd always been able to read her mind.

He frowned. 'Believe me, it's the last thing I ever thought I'd hear myself admit to anyone.'

Zoe shook her head. 'You know, don't you…? You're just saying that now because…' Her breaths came choppy and fast.

Maks frowned. 'Know what? Zoe, what is it?'

She turned away, but Maks caught her arm, turning her back. He was close. Too close.

'Zoe, what the hell is going on?'

The words tumbled out—finally. 'I *am* pregnant, Maks. I lied in London because it was too much, seeing you in my flat. You were saying that stuff about me colluding with Dean, and I couldn't believe you still didn't trust me, and I just… I was so hurt. I couldn't tell you then.' She stopped.

Maks was looking at her. His face stripped bare of expression. She saw when her words sank in. He let her arm go. Stood back.

'You are pregnant?'

She nodded, and braced herself for his inevitable reaction, in spite of what he'd just said. Surely the reality would remind him of how he really felt… But what she saw was dawning anger.

'When *were* you going to tell me? After you'd had the baby? When it was three months old? The way Nikos had to find out about *his* son?'

'No. I don't know. I was going to tell you soon… I just…'

How could she articulate what she'd been afraid of?

First that he would reject his unborn child and now that he would reject *her*?

'Maks, I'm sorry. I should have told you that day in London.'

He looked at her for a long moment, a slightly shell-shocked expression on his face, and then he said, 'This changes everything.'

Zoe looked wary. 'What do you mean?'

'We're a family now.'

Zoe was shaking her head. 'No, we're not. That's a ridiculous thing to say.'

So why did it make treacherous hope bloom?

She thought of something and hope dissolved. 'I saw those photos of you in Paris with your brothers. That's why I held back from telling you even when you arrived here. I read the speculation in the papers that you're all under pressure to settle down and prove that the Marchetti Group is stable. That's why you've suddenly decided that maybe it wouldn't be a bad thing if I was pregnant, isn't it?'

Maks shook his head, as if that would make Zoe's words make sense. He had no idea what she was talking about. And then he remembered. That drink in Paris with his brothers. Someone had taken surreptitious pictures with their phone and sold them to the tabloids.

'No, Zoe. *No.* That's not what happened.'

But she wasn't listening. She was backing away again.

'I won't do it, Maks. I won't pretend to be a happy family when we both know it would be a lie. You came here to rekindle an affair, not to make a family. I won't let you use our baby like this.'

Maks was still reeling at the news that she was pregnant. Reeling and filled with something else—something that was spreading out to every cell in his body, filling him with resolve.

'Zoe, I came here because I couldn't stay away. You've haunted me for over a month. I can't look at another woman.'

She shook her head. 'That's just lust. You don't want a family. Stop pretending you're okay with this.'

All the jagged edges that had rubbed inside Maks all his life were finally slotting into place. He just had to convince Zoe.

He thought of something and pointed out, 'We didn't use protection just now.'

Zoe looked confused, and then understanding sank in. She blushed.

Maks said, 'If your cycle is regular, and if you weren't already pregnant, then I think it's safe to say we took a great risk today. It didn't even occur to me to use protection, because when I'm with you I can't think straight. I want you so badly that all the things I thought I believed in and wanted suddenly don't matter any more. You're the only thing that matters.'

Zoe wasn't sure what Maks was saying, but walls were collapsing and dissolving inside her. Walls she'd erected long ago to keep pain out. Walls that had also kept joy out.

Emotion rose before she could stem it. Emotion she'd been suppressing for years. For ever.

Brokenly, she said, 'I can't have a family, Maks. I won't do it.'

He came close. Too close. 'Then why didn't you just get rid of the baby if you feel so strongly about it?'

The very thought made her feel sick. She put a hand on her belly. 'I never even contemplated doing that.'

'So you're happy to have it be just you and the baby?'

Zoe nodded. She could manage that. She couldn't manage more. She couldn't manage what Maks seemed to be suggesting with his presence, and with a look in his eyes that sent far too dangerous yearnings deep into her soul, where she knew what she wanted but was too scared to articulate it out loud.

Maks shook his head. 'That's not how this is going to work. I won't let you keep my child from me, Zoe.'

'But you never even wanted a child.'

'That was before it was a reality. That's before I realised that I didn't actually know what I wanted.'

Zoe didn't want to ask the question, but the words fell out of her mouth. 'What *do* you want?'

'You,' Maks said simply. 'Us.' He put a hand down on hers over her tiny, barely there bump. *'This.'*

'Why are you saying this?'

Maks's steel-grey gaze locked onto hers. 'You don't get it yet?'

She shook her head, terrified of the emotion simmering too close to the surface, threatening to break free.

He smiled, and Zoe was almost too distracted to notice that it lacked his customary confidence.

'I love you, Zoe. I came here to pursue an affair, but deep down I knew that there was no way I could let you go again. I knew I wanted more than that. And it's not just because of the baby. I won't lie and say it'll be easy. It won't. The thought of being a father terrifies me. But I know I want to do it differently from my father. I want to give my child all the love and support I never had.'

Hot moisture prickled behind Zoe's eyes. She desperately tried to stem the flow, but her cheeks were wet before she even realised she couldn't stop the tears. Silent sobs racked her body.

Maks cursed and pulled her into his chest, wrapping his arms around her, holding her tight. Not letting go even though Zoe clenched her fists against him, as if that could stop him offering comfort.

He said gruffly, 'I'm not letting go, Zoe. Ever.'

When the storm had passed, and Zoe was numb from the release of emotion, she pulled back. Maks looked down and cupped her face, wiping her cheeks with his thumbs. She sniffed. She could only imagine what a sight she looked. Puffy eyes. Puffy cheeks.

'Do you really mean it?'

Maks's mouth quirked. 'That I love you? Yes, I do. The whole damn world knows it too, if they care to look at my expression in that photo rather than at the rest of my body.'

Zoe realised she'd seen it that day, through her viewfinder, but she'd been too scared to believe it for a second.

'I know you love me too, Zoe. So don't try and deny it.'

She looked up at Maks. A sense of futility washed through her. She did love him. She'd loved him from the moment she'd trusted him enough to let him make love to her.

Still, something stubborn inside her made her resist taking the final leap of faith. She said, 'It's just the baby.'

Maks shook his head. 'No, you don't get to use the baby as an excuse not to trust me, Zoe.'

'But how can we do this after everything we've been through? I'm scared, Maks. Scared to allow myself to love you or to feel happy. Because I know how quickly it can be snatched away.'

And because she didn't deserve it.

Maks raised a brow. 'Is that a good enough excuse to half-live your life? In a perpetual state of fear and misplaced guilt?'

She looked up at Maks, but before she could respond he said, 'There's something else you need to know. I meant to tell you earlier…but you distracted me.'

'What?'

'You've never looked up anything about the crash in the press, have you?'

Zoe shuddered at the thought. 'No, why would I?'

'So you've never known that the reason your father crashed wasn't because he was distracted. It was because a couple of joy-riding kids had stolen a car and were driving on the wrong side of the road…'

Zoe searched Maks's face for signs that he was just making this up. But the faintest glimmer of a memory was coming back to her. People talking in hushed voices as they looked at her with pity. She'd blocked out so much of that time, and she'd been so young…and then she'd never wanted to think about it.

That moment when her father had looked back at

her just before the crash had been crystallised in her mind, but maybe...

'Zoe, even if he'd had his eyes on the road he wouldn't have had a chance. It was too narrow to escape them. You need to know that. It wasn't your fault.'

This was huge. Too huge to take in fully right now. But even as she thought that she felt something shift inside her, like a knot loosening.

Maks said, 'We're different, Zoe. Things can be different for us. I'm willing to take the risk if you are.'

Could she do it? Hand herself over to this man whom she loved but didn't have the guts to say it out loud to yet?

And then it hit her. She simply didn't have a choice except to move forward. For the sake of their baby as much as for her own sake. That was why she'd come back here. That was why she'd never contemplated anything but having her baby.

Maks turned her around to face the water and wrapped one arm around her while pointing out to sea with the other. The clouds were parting to reveal blue sky. And a rainbow.

He said, close to her ear, 'We can't do anything but trust in each other and weather whatever comes our way, but I wouldn't want to do it with anyone else. I love you.'

The rainbow shimmered and glistened, beckoning her to put her trust in this man. She had a sense of her family around her, urging her on. Urging her to finally let go of the guilt that had dogged her whole life. The guilt that she'd used like a shield to stop herself from getting hurt.

It hadn't been her fault.

Zoe felt a sense of peace wash over her. Acceptance. And a rush of love so intense that she turned around, rose up on her toes and wrapped her arms around Maks's neck.

She'd thought it would be hard to say the words, but in the end it was the easiest thing in the world. 'I love you, Maks.'

'Say that again.'

'I love you.'

Joy flooded her being when she saw the awe she felt reflected in Maks's eyes.

He said, 'Will you marry me? Not for the baby or for any other reason except that I know I want to spend the rest of my life with you and I want everyone to know you're mine. And because I love you.'

Zoe bit her lip, scarcely believing what she was hearing. Slivers of lingering fear and guilt—for wanting what her parents had had and hoping that her life could be different—that it wouldn't be cut so tragically short-threatened to rise and drown her again.

But Maks brushed her hair back and said, 'I know, Zoe. I get it. I'm scared too—believe me. I only saw meanness and selfishness. I'm afraid I don't know how to be a good father. But I know I wouldn't want to do this with anyone else. So will you? Marry me and take the biggest risk of your life?'

The fear and guilt receded, banished finally by the naked emotion she saw in Maks's eyes. A giddy happiness flooded her whole body.

Zoe smiled through her tears. 'Yes, I will. I love you, Maks.'

The risk was huge, but she knew that the reward would be even greater.

He covered her mouth with his, taking her breath and taking her soul and her heart for ever.

EPILOGUE

Four years later. London.

'THERE'S MAMA! LOOK!'

Maks hushed his three-and-a-half-year-old daughter Luna as they walked into the huge, cavernous studio where the photo-shoot was taking place.

'Yes, I see her, *piccolina*. But we can't say hello just yet—she's working.'

'Okay, Papa.'

His daughter wrapped her arms around his neck and buried her head in his neck, and his heart swelled at the easy, instinctive gesture.

Luna had eyes that were an unusual mix of green and grey, and dark blond hair like her father.

Never, not for a moment, did Maks take the love of his daughter or his wife for granted.

Zoe looked around at that moment, saw them, and smiled. Her hair was up in a loose topknot. She never used it to hide her face any more. She sent them a small wave and a kiss. Maks sent her an explicit look that she clearly recognised, and when she blushed in response, he smirked. Even as his own body reacted to that blush. Still.

Time and the reality of family life, terrifying and exhilarating all at once, hadn't dimmed their desire or their love. It had only compounded it, turning it into something Maks had never believed existed. Trust. Harmony. Endless love.

Zoe turned back to finish photographing the model for a magazine cover. The model was striking—one of the hottest at the moment. Zoe had actually spotted her on the street and nurtured her herself. Originally a refugee from Angola, the girl was stunningly beautiful, yet her face was marked with the scars of war. But she wore them proudly and they'd become a trademark of her look, thanks to Zoe.

Pride filled Maks as he watched his wife at work. There was a quiet buzz of activity in the studio, but also a serenity—a trademark of Zoe's method. She'd already made a name for herself as one of the world's most in-demand photographers, but what had earned her even more respect was the fact that she'd insisted on working her way up through the ranks. Biding her time and learning with the greats. Not using her contacts to get ahead.

Once people had become aware that she was *the* Stephen Collins's daughter, which had inevitably come out once their engagement had been announced, the press had had a field-day rehashing old stories of the tragic crash and her glamorous lineage. And that vast inheritance. But they'd weathered the public interest together, until it had died down again.

* * *

Finally, Zoe was done. She loved knowing that Maks and Luna were here, waiting for her. She never felt fully at peace unless she was close to them. She said her goodbyes to her team and the rest of the crew, and to Sara, the model, who had become a good friend.

Zoe only worked with companies and models that promoted an alternative view of the fashion industry. She knew that locked her out of a lot of lucrative work, but she wasn't doing it to make money. She was doing it because she loved it.

Everything in her life was motivated by love now. And nothing more so than her love for her family.

She walked to Maks and Luna, sliding into their arms like a missing jigsaw piece. Luna's small arms wrapped around her neck and Zoe took her, pressing kisses all over her face, making her giggle.

Maks pulled her close, glancing down at her very distended belly. 'Please tell me now you're officially on maternity leave?' He sounded mildly exasperated.

She'd been due to take maternity leave a few weeks ago, but jobs had kept enticing her back. She smiled up at Maks and wrapped her free arm around his waist. He was in full protective Alpha male mode, and she had to admit she found it beyond sexy.

'Yes, finally. And I need a foot rub so bad…'

He smiled, and it was wicked. 'Just a foot rub?'

To Zoe's chagrin, she blushed. Still! After all this time.

She smiled back. 'You're insatiable.'

Maks affected a wounded look. 'Me? I seem to re-call this morning that you were the one—'

'When is Ben going to come?'

Luna's small voice interrupted their private moment.

Zoe looked at her daughter and her heart swelled. 'In a couple of weeks, sweetie, when he's ready.'

They were having a son, and had decided to call him Ben, after her brother.

Luna clapped her hands. 'Can we go and buy him some presents?'

Zoe sent Maks a dry look. Their daughter was far too smart for her own good. She'd figured out that presents for the baby meant presents for her too.

Maks plucked her out of Zoe's arms. '*One* present—*if* you eat all your dinner tonight and go to bed early and let Hamish read you a story.'

'With his funny voice?'

'With his funny voice.'

Maks took Zoe's hand and lifted it, kissing the palm of her hand while Luna chattered on happily.

Their life was about to expand and get even more hectic. If Zoe stopped to think for a moment she felt breathless. This much love? This much happiness? It was a risk, for sure, but it was a risk she would take over and over again. Because the reward was beyond anything she could ever have imagined.

'Home?' Maks asked.

Zoe looked up and saw their world reflected in his loving gaze. She deserved this. They both did. And everything would be fine.

She smiled. 'Home.'

* * * * *

WE HOPE YOU ENJOYED
THIS BOOK FROM
⟨H⟩HARLEQUIN
PRESENTS

Escape to exotic locations where passion knows no bounds.

Welcome to the glamorous lives of royals and billionaires,
where passion knows no bounds. Be swept into a world
of luxury, wealth and exotic locations.

8 NEW BOOKS AVAILABLE EVERY MONTH!

HPHALO2020

COMING NEXT MONTH FROM

H HARLEQUIN
PRESENTS

Available December 29, 2020

#3873 THE COST OF CLAIMING HIS HEIR
The Delgado Inheritance
by Michelle Smart
Blindsided by a shocking family secret, Emiliano Delgado spends one wildly passionate night with fiery Becky Aldridge. But as he's cursing himself for breaching his boundaries, Becky has life-changing news...

#3874 WHAT THE GREEK'S WIFE NEEDS
by Dani Collins
Tanja's whirlwind marriage to billionaire Leon Patrakis has been over since he returned to Greece five years ago... Yet, to keep the baby she's adopting, Tanja has a last request: they stay wed...in name only!

#3875 THE SECRETS SHE MUST TELL
Lost Sons of Argentina
by Lucy King
Finn Calvert is reeling from the shocking revelation that he has a son with lawyer Georgie Wallace! He's determined to step up as a father but as their chemistry reignites, he learns there are more secrets to be unveiled...

#3876 CHOSEN FOR HIS DESERT THRONE
by Caitlin Crews
Sheikh Tarek's kingdom needs a queen. And discovering a beautiful prisoner in his palace only puts the nation closer to the brink of collapse. Until he realizes Dr. Anya Turner might just be the key he's looking for...